From Pegs to Pens

Written by
Michelle Burton, Alison Killeen,
Gemma Middleton and Amanda Stone

First published in 2006 by Lulu.com

Copyright © 2006 Middleton, Stone, Killeen, Burton.

All rights reserved.

ISBN 978-1-84753-814-7

'This book is dedicated to all our families'

Acknowledgements

A special thank you to Mimi Thebo for all her support, encouragement and enthusiasm. Thanks also to Steve May and the staff at Bath Spa University, including Barbara Bloomfield who edited this book. We would like to acknowledge Catherine Lumsden and Rebecca Burton for all their help. As well as co-writing this book, Alison Killeen illustrated the front cover.

Alison, Amanda, Gemma & Michelle.

CONTENTS

Acknowledgements

All About Me – Gemma Middleton   8

Fiction: From Pegs to Pens

Mr King: 11
Hush Little Baby: 16
Role-Play: 21
A Day in the Life: 25
Appearances: 32
Train Accident in a Far Away Place: 34
Gathering of the Clan: 36
The Odd One Out: 37
The Swimming Pool Incident: 40
Colour of the Day: 45
The Wiccan Way: 49
Enjoying the Ride: 60
The Amanda Show: 61
It is Worse: 69
Settee: 70
Picture Perfect: 72
Chocolate Chip Muffin: 74
Worth the Risk?:   76
The Frog Prince: 77
After: 80
Extract from the unpublished novel 'Hiding':   86
Revenge is a Dish Best Served Cold: 95
Stars: 98
Meaning of Life: 99
The Homecoming: 100
Being a Grown up: 102

All About the Creative Writing Course: 105

Articles: Pressed Items

Leaving Home: 107
Our Story: 110
PND – The Silent Illness: 116
An African Container: 121
Treat the Habit or Punish the Crime?:   124
Sleep Deprivation: 127
Rebel With a Menopause: 131

All About Me – Michelle Burton   133

Life Writing: Dirty Linen

The Afterbirth: 136
Childhood: 138
A Stranger's Gift: 147
My Father: 150
My Childhood Memory: 153
Chicken Noodle Soup: 156
The Bothy: 158
Living the Life: 160
Solange: 169
A Good Night Out: 176
Why Didn't I Tell Him: 178
Bath: 180

All About Me – Alison Killeen   183

Script for Radio: Brighter Whites

Always Look on the Bright Side of Life: 186

All About Me – Amanda Stone   203

Poetry: The Comfort of Ariel

<u>Nature</u>
Nature in Periphery: 207
Her: 208
Hamster: 209
Sunset: 210
Remembrance: 211

<u>Invisible strings</u>
Telling Them: 213
Tread Softly: 214
You, Me and Your Epilepsy: 215
You: 216
Evening Meal: 217

<u>The Darker Side</u>
The Waiting Room: 219
My Best Friend: 220
Patience: 221
Aged: 222
Wordless: 223
My Needs: 224
Time: 226
The Funeral Home: 227
Necessity: 228

<u>Woman</u>
Woman: 229
24 Hours: 230
My Place: 231
A Thank You to Austen: 233

<u>Childhood</u>
Large Alien: 234

Childhood: 235
Boy with the Blue Eyes: 236
Shoes: 237
Boyhood: 238
Cease-Fire: 239

All About Me

Well, what can I tell you about me that won't send you to sleep? I live in Keynsham with my partner and our two children. I am 33-years-old and before returning to education I worked as a hairdresser, support worker, mental health care assistant and a drink and drug counsellor. I left school at 16 with no formal qualifications and started training as a hairdresser (where I rivalled Edward Scissorhands.) I skipped from one career to another until I finally decided to put my heart into what I enjoyed doing most…writing. At 27, I enrolled at my local college and started studying for my GCSEs. I rediscovered the joys of learning and continued until I had enough qualifications to go to university. I am now in my final year studying for a Bachelor of Arts in Creative Writing and Drama. Are you still awake?

My stories, poetry and life writing are influenced by my own beliefs, experience and the many different characters I have met during my life. Most of my poetry is taken from my career as a counsellor and the amazing people I liaised with during this time. They showed me what strength really means. Some of my life writing is based on my own childhood and the fiction comes from a vivid imagination and a bizarre sense of humour.

I took part in writing this book firstly because writing is my passion, and secondly to encourage anyone who has a dream to pursue it. It is never too late to and all you need is a belief in yourself and determination. Happy reading.

Gemma Middleton

From Peg to Pens

Mr King

Mr King liked biscuits. He especially liked chocolate ones, the kind that melted into his coffee when he dunked them. Mr King also liked murder. Any kind of murder.

He would scan the papers like a vulture, feeding on stories of other people's demise. The more horrific, the better fed he felt. Mr King had been known to visit murder scenes. He had taken part in searches for missing people, desperate to be the one to locate the body. He wished he could find them lying cold, lifeless and preferably naked. It was not for a safe return that he gave up his spare time to rummage about in cold, muddy fields, getting stung and scratched. Oh no, he was on his own mission. But so far his searches had never proved fruitful. He had never been lucky enough to *see* a dead body. Well, unless you counted his mother, and she had died peacefully in her sleep, so, in his eyes, she was out of the equation. And she looked peaceful. Now that was something he did not want to see again.

He wanted to feel blood on his hands. He wanted to see the eyes of his victim staring up at him, begging for a reprieve. "Don't kill me!" he heard them scream, "I will do anything…" He wanted to feel a power unlike any he could imagine. Mr King was going to kill.

But there was one slight problem with Mr King's quest. Victims. He was not a man who spent time in public, nor did he have a wide circle of friends. In fact, one could be forgiven for referring to him as a loner. He had read profiles of killers, written by experts who 'got inside their head.' Most murders were carried out by someone the victim knew and Mr King did not really know *anybody*. The idea of socializing terrified him. No, he would have to find victims some other way, and Mr King spent many a cold afternoon pondering the problem of 'victim location.'

He would not be an average serial killer. Sexual pleasure was not on his agenda. He had no intention of performing a rape. Mr King liked the idea of a naked victim, but only because he thought the victim would feel vulnerable without clothes. His victims were not going to die holding on to their dignity. Oh no, they were going to die begging for mercy, begging him, Mr King, for their life, and if they begged for their clothes back, then that was even better. Inside his mind, Mr King made a mental challenge to the so-called experts to profile him. Let them try and categorize him. He was un-categorize-able. Unique. A self taught expert in the field of murder.

Mr King was a book keeper for a small garage. He worked from home in his spare room-cum-study, and he only saw his employers weekly when he collected their receipts. Mr King's employers thought he was odd. Mr King knew but this did not bother him in the slightest. He was not here to be liked. He was here to carry out his mission. For 16 years, Mr King and his employers had enjoyed no conversation lasting more than a few minutes. Mr King had decided that he needed to find a new work place. Somewhere that would be useful in his 'victim location.' So, for the next three months Mr King scanned the jobs section intently. Instead of dissecting stories of gore and murder, his quest for a job became his new obsession. This was step one towards his goal, each goal listed and ticked as he achieved them. Just for the morbidly curious amongst you, his list looked like this:

- Find Job
- Locate victim

- Plan murder
- Carry out plan
- Cover all tracks

Within six months, Mr King was on step four.

Mr King watched, studied and learned. He congratulated himself on his own cleverness. He was on schedule, and more importantly, he was unstoppable. Now, he thought, I will be the one in charge. The one with power, holding all the cards. The one with blood on his hands. For Mr King, all his dreams were coming true.

He walked to the hut with a smile on his face. This was it. On entering the hut, Mr King swallowed. The smell. He could still not get used to the stench, despite weeks of walking through the hut. Victims had a certain aroma, he thought, of waiting to die. He scanned his potential victims, each one looking back at him, speaking with their eyes, but saying nothing. They knew, he thought. They knew it was just a matter of time. If it wasn't today, then it might be tomorrow. Until then, they would stay in the hut and wait. Wait for Mr King, the all powerful one, to decide who would be next.

Mr King spent time deliberating. His first would be special. He knew that, and would not rush this special moment for anything. You never forget the first, he thought, and when he looked into piercing blue eyes, he knew he had found what he wanted.

He had to drag her from the hut. He had tied the string around her neck, but it was still a battle of the strongest. She was not going voluntarily. She let out a grunt. A grunt of fear and distress, but Mr King just kept on dragging.

He got her into his 'workshop' (as he had named it) and spent a few minutes admiring what he saw. Her naked flesh glistened from the light coming through one small window. He could see the hairs standing up, maybe from cold, maybe from fear. He marvelled at her nakedness, seeing no beauty, only vulnerability. As he removed the string from her neck, both looked at the door. But Mr King was quick. Quick thinking and quick acting. He slammed her only means of escape shut, with a force that told her he would not be gentle.

Mr King lifted her up and was amazed at her heaviness. He wanted her on his table, laid there for him. She was not struggling much now. Mr King forced her head towards him. He wanted her to see a master at work. In his hand he held his implement of death, a shiny-bladed tool that would penetrate her flesh, and allow the fluid beneath to spill freely over him. Oh, how he wanted that moment, but still being the ever practical Mr King, he had on a thick leather apron to protect his new slacks. He had even made sure to dress for the occasion.

He pulled her head up hard, and she made that funny grunting sound again. Her neck was exposed, the vein throbbing against the force of his hold. He raised his knife and felt the rush of excitement course through him. Years of waiting and months of planning had finally brought him to this special moment. He smiled, and slit her throat.

He had to be quick with the next stage. The hook dangled from the ceiling. In fact, there were many hooks lined up. He had cleaned those hooks only this morning, polishing them until they gleamed. He spent a few seconds binding her legs, and with an abundance of blood still pouring from her slashed throat, he roughly lowered the hook and gouged a big hole, via the backbone, until she was skewered firmly through to the stomach. She was upside down and bleeding from two wounds. Mr King firmly hoisted the hook until she was eight feet off the ground.

Mr King sighed. He allowed himself some time to bask in his own glory. It had been everything he had expected, and more. He kept glancing over at her, to reassure himself that it had not been a dream. He really had committed his first murder, and she was still there, dangling and bleeding as proof of his achievement. He did not hear the door open.

"You did it then?" The voice said, looking over at Mr King's first victim.

"A neat job too."

Mr King looked up, saying nothing, his shining eyes telling all.

"Well done, Mr King. You will fit in well in my abattoir."

Gemma Middleton

Hush Little Baby

She is sleeping. Her arms are above her head in an unfinished stretch. Her tiny fingers are motionless. If I listen really hard I can just hear her breathing. Her chest is moving slowly up and down. She is so beautiful. Her eyelashes are long and soft, like a chick's downy feathers. Trapped in the corner of her eye is a big round tear, left over from earlier. When she was crying it felt as if every nerve in my body was tensed. I could feel panic beginning to rise in me as I desperately tried to work out what she wanted. But now she is sleeping and I am at peace. I feel so relaxed that part of me wants to crawl into bed and sleep, but I won't. I will stay to be near my precious baby girl.

Hush, little baby, don't say a word; Mama's going to buy you a mockingbird.

When we first married, we decided to wait before having a baby. For the first year it felt as if our lives had collided. We had separate routines and trying to live as a couple meant that we inevitably had rows. Replacing the empty toilet roll became a big issue as did whose turn it was to cook. But eventually, with time, we began to skilfully side-step each other's moods and a daily pattern was established. It was then that we decided to start a family. We were full of anticipation. Trying boys' and girls' names out, weaving them with our surname to see how they would sound. Eliminating names that could make a child vulnerable to playground taunts. We would walk around Mothercare and look at prams. I was like a five-year-old waiting for Christmas and that special gift.

And if that mockingbird don't sing, Mama's going to buy you a diamond ring.

Each month I would feel a familiar dull ache in my back and gnawing pain in my stomach. The disappointment would consume me. He would try to cheer me up by saying it would mean we got to practise more and that it would happen but we needed to relax and stop thinking about it. But the more I tried, the harder it was. Everywhere I went there were pregnant women. I was surrounded by young girls with swollen stomachs that protruded from over the tops of their designer jeans. They were not much more than children themselves. It seemed so wrong. I wanted to feel the skin stretching tight and my stomach swelling. I wanted a baby.

And if that diamond ring turns brass, Mama's going to buy you a looking glass.

After six months I thought we should go to the doctor's but he wouldn't hear of it. He kept saying that we hadn't given it long enough. His enthusiasm seemed to have dimmed and talk of doctors left him cold. So I decided to take my own action. I went to the library and fetched books. There were plenty of things we could try. I subtly changed what we ate, adding more green veg, saying it was a new diet. I bought him boxer shorts and said flattering words about finding them sexy. These things he seemed to accept but the chart and temperature checking I knew he wouldn't understand. So I hid them in the spare room wardrobe. I had spent hours and the charts were as detailed as a piece of GCSE coursework. I knew exactly when I was most fertile and would put all my effort into getting us to make love at just the right time. This went on for a couple of months until he found the thermometer and chart. He went mad, I knew he wouldn't be keen on the idea but I hadn't expected this reaction. He worked out why on some days I had a healthy appetite for sex and said he felt used. I didn't really understand what I had done that was so wrong, wasn't a baby what we both wanted? He looked at me and said "No it's what you want."

And if that looking glass gets broke, Mama's going to buy you a Billy goat.

For ages we didn't talk; there was hushed silence and weighty looks. In the end I agreed that I would stop the temperature thing and we would forget about a baby for the time being. But I didn't start taking my pill again. But nothing happened and after three weeks he announced that he needed some time away, some space. He promised me that it was only a trial separation, just some time for him to get his head together. Of course I was upset but realised that the baby thing was probably getting to him as well. Possibly sometime apart would do us both good. We would be more relaxed when he came back and I was bound to get pregnant. So I stayed reasonably cheery the day he went, saying that I would keep his side of the bed warm. It was as if he was going away on a course, not leaving me.

And if that Billy goat won't pull, Mama's going to buy a cart and bull.

When I came in from work the house seemed so empty. I would sit on the sofa and listen to the traffic passing outside, listen to other people's lives. Some evenings it would be so quiet I could hear my own heart beating. I would go up to the spare room and just sit. If I looked out, I could see children playing and laughing, their world so simple, so full of life. Then I had the idea of decorating the room. When he came home I would get pregnant straight away so by doing the room now it was one less thing to worry about. I spent evenings planning, working out colours. I decided on painting a border of chicks, a nice soft yellow to keep it unisex. Most nights I worked late and it was good going to bed exhausted.

And if that cart and bull turn over, Mama's going to buy you a dog named Rover.

Once the room was finished I started to linger round the aisles that sold the baby stuff. If things were on offer I would buy them. It seemed sensible to be prepared. I would place them in a plastic box with a lid, trapping in little puffs of air. I bought tiny white Babygros and socks that would just hold the tips of my fingers. Taking them out of their packaging, I would gently wrap them in white tissue paper. Smoothing them in the drawers, I would hear the gentle crinkle and get a real satisfaction from how crisp it felt. Soon the shelves were full of boxes and the drawers bursting with bundles of clothes.

And if that dog named Rover won't bark, Mama's going to buy you a horse and cart.

The separation slipped from days into weeks. I hadn't phoned sooner because I wanted to give him space. But every time the phone rang I would rush to answer it, hoping that it would be him. But it never was. In the end I decided to call but his mobile was turned off. He hadn't told me where he was staying.

And if that horse and cart fall down, you'll still be the sweetest little baby in town.

They came at about half past four this afternoon, banging on the door. They were hitting it with great big blows which made the glass vibrate. It was hardly surprising that she began to cry loud, stinging cries that were cloaked by their shouts. Then someone pushed past me and ran upstairs. They were so loud and rough. It was all so confusing, and I couldn't understand what was happening. Then a policewoman came down the stairs carrying her, she was saying: "Let's go and find your mum'. I tried to tell her that she wouldn't be able to because her mum had gone. She had left her in the petrol station. But no one was listening to me.

They took me to the police station and kept asking me questions about when and where I found her, I explained that she had been left. I couldn't work out what was going on. Everything started to confuse me. Then they started to call me a baby snatcher. I explained to them that she was just left alone in the car. It was so cold and she was so cold. Someone had to look after her. I did look for her mother but I couldn't see her, so I brought her home. I just wanted to look after her. Then they asked me if I had hurt her in any way. She had been left and I took care of her, not hurt her. Then they said that she wasn't left, her mother was paying for petrol. They had checked the petrol station's security tapes, she was gone for no more than three minutes and they could see I hadn't looked for the woman. I don't understand. I did try and find her. The baby was all alone. Just like me. I was going to look after her.

She was my baby and then my husband would come home. And we would be a proper family.

Alison Killeen

Role-Play
I

His eyes, like hot pools of melted chocolate, smoulder with barely contained desire. His thick, strong arms grasp her waist, as his lips lower towards her own...

"Mum! Mum! Ellie took my Barbie, the one with the purple stripes in her hair and the skirt that you said was more like a belt." Whining and audible lip quivering. "And she's my *favourite*! Mum! Mum!"

"Umm, yes honey, ok. In a minute"

"But Mum!" Angry sounding now. "You're not listening!" Stamp, followed by retreating footfalls. From the next room: "Mum says you've got to give it back!"

She held her breath, as their lips met and he pulled her towards him. Her heart raced as she felt the force of his passion against her and the heat of his body next to her...

"Mum! She's lying! I had it first; she put it down when she went for a wee." Self-righteous anger and hands on hips. Mumbling. "Not fair, she's just picking on me".

Eyes determinedly closed, "Yes Laura, in a minute."

"But Mum! I'm not Laura, I'm Ellie!" Tugging of parental sleeve. "I knew you loved her more than me!" Pout.

Anna sighs, resignedly opening her eyes and replacing her spectacles. "I'm sorry, of course you're Ellie" she soothes, lifting her daughter onto her lap and pushing the hair out of the tiny, aggrieved face. "And you know I love you both the same."

No chance of enjoying a little extracurricular fantasy fun now. Glancing at the clock, Anna calculates that the girls have managed to play peaceably for a total of seven minutes. Time to prepare dinner then.

II

His lips brushed against her neck, his hot breath warming her skin. She shuddered with anticipation, as his mouth began to explore her collarbone and continued southward...

"Arrrgghh!" Anna is thrust back into reality as burning pain sears at her hand. Looking down, her right hand is covered in bolognaise sauce. "Shit," she mutters, hastily removing the pan from the heat and running her hand under the cold tap.

"Mummy! You said a bad word!"

Thinking at maximum mummy-speed, Anna declares: "No darling, Mummy said 'shoot'".

"No you didn't"

Turning off the tap, Anna looks into her daughter's stubborn eyes, lowering her voice to that particular level that any child would recognise as a warning, *"Ellie!"*

Ellie opts for a swift exit, stage right (aka, the backdoor), muttering as she goes. Guilt nibbles at Anna's conscience. Bloody stereotypical frustrated housewife! She busies herself with locating the pack of quick-cook spaghetti.

III

7.36 and the girls are bathed, fairytaled and tucked up under duvets covered with scantily-clad Barbies. Anna pours herself a big glass of red wine as she subconsciously switches from full mummy-duty to intuitive low-frequency radar alert. Defcon one.

Anna sinks into the sofa, snuggling into the corner and tucking her feet beneath her. She gently closes her eyes and allows herself to be lulled by the tones of Nina Simone. Peace at last.

Anna becomes aware that Nina wants someone to put some 'Sugar in [Her] Bowl'. A small smile appears on her lips, as she hits the memory rewind button. Oh yes! Hot breath. Southward.

Meanwhile, his fingers deftly unbutton her blouse. Her body arches toward him, hungry for his lips to ensnare her rousing peaks. He holds back, tantalisingly, running his tongue around her...

"I want a drink". Startled, Anna is yanked back to her living room and the demands of an insomniac six-year-old. Stepford-mummy smile in place, she provides water and returns escapee to Pepto Bismol-coloured holding cell.

IV

Wrapped in her too-good-to-wear, optimistic/surprise-Christmas-present-from-spouse, red silk robe, Anna enters the lounge and turns the lights to low. She downs her wine and replenishes the empty glass, placing and filling a second glass next to her own. She arranges herself on the sofa, and waits.

Twenty-three minutes and eleven seconds later (Anna's eyes have been glued to the clock on the DVD player), Anna hears the front door opening, and husband, John, enters the room moments later. "I've had a bloody awful day. God, it's gloomy in here. Suppose its spag bol again for dinner?" Silence eventually catches his attention. "Hey, isn't that the robe I got you for Christmas? Thought you were never going to wear it!" Realisation dawns at last and he leers towards her. "Hey, Momma, someone needs an appointment with the lurrrve doctor." As his eyes crawl over her exposed thigh, he continues his romantic advances with: "Red Riding Hood wants a visit from the woodsman. She wants to play with his chopper!"

Resisting the urge to gag her lothario, Anna puts her finger to his lips. "Sssshhh!" she breathes, expertly veiling impatience with ardour. She unties the sash of her robe, revealing her nakedness beneath. As John rises to the challenge, Anna slips her glasses from her nose. All the better *not* to see you with, she smiles to herself.

Amanda Stone

A day in the life…

I have truly excelled myself today. I have gone beyond my own boundaries in the realms of stupidity and in eight hours, I have lost an eyebrow, a job and my self respect. Start at the beginning…

It's 7.30 am and I have a job interview. I want this job. Correction, NEED this job as it is going to put me back in the league of 'professional working mum.' All my friends have children, loving partner and a career, managing all with the ease and dexterity that I can only dream about. I, on the other hand, fight with my partner, arrive late for my poxy job in Tesco and possess children that rival any witnessed on 'Supernanny.' This job is going to give me self respect and the respect of my anally retentive super-loving-super-working-super-mum friends. So I guess you all get the gist of why I need this job.

It is only 7.30 you may think, lots of time to prepare for any interview. But in my household getting out the front door on time takes the planning of a military exercise. I have to be at the bank (where said interview is to take place) by 10 o'clock. I am hoping to walk out with the new job description of 'bank clerk' complete with plans to progress and become as high up as little old me can climb within the branch (and all without having to sleep with anyone.) A mammoth task, but one I have mentally prepared for since becoming a mother. Before any of this can happen I have to get the children safely off to school. Um, just repeating all this back to you is causing shudders. Why did I not do things differently? James has already undressed himself twice. It's always the same. I dress him, he undresses, and the cycle repeats until one of us wins. This is normally me Mondays to Fridays, but not always and today is one of those 'not always' days. I have threatened him with everything from 'wait till your father gets home' to foster care, but nothing is working. I'm sure the little darling has psychic powers and *knows* I want everything to run smoothly today. As I am walking towards the kitchen to prepare sandwiches I pick up one sock, a school shirt and a pair of pants. All other items of attire appear to be missing and James is now in the lounge, naked and jumping up and down on his brother who is threatening violence.

    I look at the clock mocking me above the fireplace and notice it is already 8.01 am. I have 35 minutes before I have to leave or my schedule becomes a pile of poo. At this point words from my best friend, Alice, leap annoyingly into my head. 'All professional people must have a schedule and stick to it Emma, otherwise the whole day becomes left to chance.' As my whole life has always been left to chance, this only bothers me slightly, but today is the first day of my 'professional' life and if I can't manage a schedule for half a morning, what chance have I got? After making the conscious decision to prepare packed lunches and deal with James later(I should have got up at 4am) we finally leave home at 8.45, James minus a sock and Andrew missing his hard boiled egg in his lunchbox that I didn't have enough time to cook.

    I drive to school in silence, racked with guilt and torturing myself that James will get frostbite in his toes and Andrew might develop an eating disorder during puberty. The traffic is (of course) horrendous and when I finally pull up outside the school gates the bell has already rang meaning I have to walk to the office, make up some excuse as to why my children are late and sign them in the late book. Andrew glares at me as I tell the school secretary we are late because of traffic. Andrew hates not getting somewhere on time and he looks as if he will soon cry. I know that I am now officially a bad mother. My children make up at least 95% of the names in the late book and I mentally curse the other 5% of mothers that could have been late today with me to make me feel slightly better.

During the long, slow and painful drive home I think of everything still left to do. The drive to the bank will take me at least 20 minutes so I must leave home at 9.30. It is already 9.03 am and I have to shower, dress, prepare hair to bank clerk standard and strategically apply make up in less than twenty minutes. I am doomed.

I finally pull into my drive at 9.09 and I thank God for the extra one minute he has given me. No sooner have I walked into the front door when the phone rings and dear Miss Smith is informing me that James is missing a sock and could I kindly bring it back into school for him. I picture the scene. James proudly showing off his bare foot as his teacher makes a mental note to contact social services. I resign myself to the fact that I will have to drop the bloody sock off en route and plan to auction James on eBay as soon as I get a spare minute. As I run up the stairs at a speed to rival Zola Budd I catch a glimpse of something white sitting on the top stair. James's sock. Murder is now freshly in my mind and while running the shower, removing clothes and taking out my only suit from the wardrobe I realise I also have to shave my legs as well. The bank would not allow me to even clean for them if they could see how un-organized and inefficient I really am. Please, please let me make the interview on time.

After showering and washing my hair in thirty seconds I look down at my legs that resemble a prickly 'welcome home' doormat. At this exact point I make the decision that was the catalyst for the next few hours. I decide to use hair remover on my legs instead of the razor (otherwise I end up looking like I have bodged a suicide attempt) and I successfully remove leg hair and an eyebrow. I had an itch around my eye and forgot the hair remover was still on my hands. After relieving myself of the itch, I relieved myself of an eyebrow as well and I didn't even notice until I looked at my half decent appearance that was dressed, hair dried and leg hair free. Something did not look right. I had a lop sided look about me but I couldn't work out exactly why that was until I leaned up close into the mirror trying to work out how to apply my make up like the woman at the Clarins counter in Boots did.

My heart stopped beating as I realized I resembled a stereotypical village idiot. What do I do? Remove the other one or pencil line one on in place of the missing eyebrow? I chose the latter and grabbing sock on the way out I made my way back to the school avoiding any glances in my wing mirror that could remind me of how utterly ridiculous I must look.

When I reached the school gates for the second time, I was fifteen minutes behind my impossible-to-reach schedule and might have to face the dragon again. I pressed the speaker buzzer on the wall outside the office and informed Mrs whoever (dragon did not answer buzzer) that I was Mrs Carlson and had come in to deliver my son's sock. I'm sure I heard tittering as she opened the door to me. I thrust the sock into her hands and noticed a startled glance at my face. I tried to ignore it, mumbled James name and class, jumped back into my car and drove to the bank at break neck speed. This did however gain me five minutes precious time but I still did not pull up into the bank car park until 10.08. I was now officially late, stressed, looked ridiculous and still left to endure an interview that was far beyond my reach. I wished I was just going to Tesco to sit behind a till for a few hours and had not pulled a sicky.

I tried to walk into the bank with a strategically placed hand over the missing eyebrow. I did not think how conspicuous I must have looked and as I struggled up to a free cashier to inform her I was here for an interview, I bumped my head on her glass partition. It had been partially shielded from my line of vision by my hand and I heard at least two people giggle loudly. At this point I wish I was dead. The beauty queen cashier (who would have looked good with a missing eyebrow) smirked and pointed over to some chairs. She reminded me I was late and told me I would have to wait until Mr Davids, the Manager, was free. As I sat in the posh leather-upholstered chair I tried to think of an escape plan. I decided on: faking an asthma attack, getting up and running off or pleading insanity. After intensely analyzing above-mentioned get out clauses, I decided that to fake an asthma attack might result in a ride in an ambulance, getting up and running would mean removing my hand and showing off missing eyebrow while pleading insanity was too close to the truth. Nothing for it, I had to ride it out.

After what felt like hours (in fact only 22 minutes) I had already broken a bank pen, read my stars from last December, developed an odour problem and kept my eyebrow covered the whole time. Finally, a man who introduced himself as Mr Davids came over and offered his hand. Without any time to think I shook his hand with my shield, leaving my missing eyebrow in full view. To make things even worse Mr Davids was gorgeous-looking and had the audacity to allow himself a laugh at my expense. The interview passed in a humiliating haze as Mr Davids struggled to keep his mouth from curling up and I struggled to stop the tears from flowing. I had obviously resigned myself to the fact that I was not going to get this job and all I could do was compose myself until the torture was over. It took a grand total of fifteen minutes but I can assure you it felt a lot longer. After I had walked out of the bank and was cocooned safely back in my car the tears welled up. I cried in self pity, hatred and the unfairness of it all. Mostly I cried from embarrassment.

I can now bring you back to present time. My suit has been removed and hung back in the wardrobe until the next funeral comes along. My fake eyebrow has been scrubbed off and I am sat at the kitchen table contemplating my awful day. It is 3 pm. In a few minutes I have to pick up the cherubs from school. This means facing the world again minus one eyebrow and I don't think a balaclava is a viable option. I take the coward's way out and phone Alice to ask her if she will pick them up. After only a few rings she answers the phone in a tone that tells me she has been crying.

"Hello" she snivels down the phone.

"Alice, its Emma. Are you ok?"

"Oh Em, its Pete. He…he has left me for Greta."

I hold the phone in shock. Greta is the Swedish Au pair they employed after Pete's recent promotion.

"He says he can't cope with my schedules and everything anymore. He wants to go off backpacking with Greta! I asked, what about the kids? Pete wouldn't even take a holiday last year…Oh Em, what am I going to do?"

I gave her some words of encouragement, offered to pick up her children and keep them for tea and then hung up. I drove to school in a daze. Walking up to the school playground, where no doubt both children would be up to some mischief, my missing eyebrow was furthermost from my mind. I always perceived Alice to have the perfect everything. Life, husband and career. At least my husband, Tom, would never run off with the au pair. Of course we could hardly afford to pay the electric bill, let alone a glorified slave. As I arrived I listened to the chatter around me. Children were arguing with their parents, mothers were gossiping, and not one person gave a glance in my direction. I was just part of the everyday. I fitted in. I asked myself what was so bad with my life anyway (omitting the missing eyebrow of course because any woman knows that is a tragedy.)

My two boys were sat quietly on a wall and this at first alarmed me. They normally resembled gorillas after school, swinging on anything available and rivalling any high pitched noise heard in a zoo. I walked up to them and Andrew beamed at me. James handed me a piece of paper and both the boys had written 'I love you mummy' inside. I noticed tears prick at the back of my eyes and felt so loved. I actually didn't want to change anything about my life. It was perfect. I sent the boys off to look for Rupert and Roger, Alice's children, and when they returned we walked back to the car.

James slid his little hand inside mine and talked animatedly about his day as we walked. I noticed how quiet Rupert and Roger were and realized it was not because my own children were so bad but because Alice's kids were unhappy. Although I felt such sadness for Alice I realized for the first time in a long while how lucky I was. After reaching the car I drove towards home as the boys messed around and played in the back. And then it dawned on me. This had not been the worse day of my life; it had turned out to be the best.

Gemma Middleton

Appearances

The house was just how she remembered it. The familiar white painted façade, trimmed with a frame of ivy that undulated in the breeze. A small smile formed on Anne's lips, as the cobbled path evoked memories of chalky games of hopscotch, and searches for marbles lost in the borders. As she followed the pathway, she felt leaves of rosemary, mint and lavender brush against her calves, filling the air with the scent of summer days that lasted forever.

She glanced at her neatly-manicured hands, and recalled how good it had felt to push her fingers deep into the damp, gritty compost when helping Nana pot geraniums or primroses. All at once, there came the remembered smell of earth on her fingers, and the memory of the ritualistic scrubbing to remove dirt that somehow managed to lodge under nails chewed mercilessly down to the skin.

On nearing the door, Anne noticed that the colourful clusters of flowerpots were missing from the doorstep and that the brass door knocker, polished by Nana until Anne could look at her distorted reflection in it, now hung dull and imageless; the house was not the same at all. Anne's stomach seemed to shift within her, as the thought occurred to her: Nana had been ill for longer than she had said.

Why had she not come home sooner? She ran her fingertips over the faint ridges of the green painted door, allowing nostalgia to delay her entry for just a few more heartbeats. A child once more, hiding from the looming realisation of her fears. Here, *now*, she felt incongruous, so thinly disguised in her grey tailored suit. Standing before Nana's door, she felt robbed of the confidence that her business clothes usually provided. What good was silk against the ravages of disease?

The knocker moved resentfully in her hand, one knock, two. Her breath wedged deep within her, as she found herself once more sat on a yellow plastic couch, with the doctor talking down to her from miles above, his strange, impossible words becoming more and more muted, stifled by the furious beating of her heart.

Amanda Stone

Train Accident in a Far Away Place

She held her sick baby son in her arms. She had lost track of the hours she spent pacing the sitting room floor. The heat from his tiny head had begun to make her arm hot. His little face glowed red. She gently stroked his cheek, made a shushing noise and rocked him in her arms. The television gave out a gentle mumble as the news reporter spoke. She wasn't really interested but wanted to hear another voice, to assure herself that she wasn't the only person awake in the world. There was footage of a train crash; she thought that she should feel something as she watched people being dragged from the wreckage. But all she could feel was a longing for her son to sleep. She sighed and began to move around the room once again.

He had told her that she shouldn't fuss, that he was nearly a grown man but she just couldn't help herself. She moved over to the window and looked out on the empty black streets. Maybe the television would be a good distraction? As the news came on she could see pictures of a crumpled train. Panic began to rise in her. Did he say that he was taking a train? Then she realised that it had happened in a place far away. She breathed a sigh of relief which was then replaced with a feeling of guilt. That young man, who she was watching being dragged from the train, had a mother like her. Then she heard the front door open and him stumble up the stairs. She didn't say anything. He is nearly a grown man and doesn't need his mother fussing.

When she woke the room was in darkness, apart from the television which illuminated a corner. It took her some minutes to work out where she was. She must have fallen asleep, she had been waiting.

She felt sure that he would have visited today. After all, it was her birthday. She had waited all day. It had been so long since he had bought the grandchildren to see her, but surely he would have come today. Mind you he always seemed so busy these days. She shivered. The room had gone cold. It must be quite late. As she looked over at the television she could see that there had been a nasty train accident in some far away place. It's funny, she thought, how accidents always happened in the early hours. Well, they weren't going to come now; she might as well go to bed. As she went to get out of the chair she felt a sharp pain across her chest and down her arm. It must be because she had been sat for so long. The pain would pass; she just needed to wait a bit longer.

Alison Killeen

Gathering of the Clan

Aggie brings out the tea tray, a welcome intrusion in this chasm of silence we have made for ourselves. Her bright smile and fresh apron are a focus for our murmurings – something to look at and draw attention from the issue that needs to be confronted and resolved. The hollow porcelain hum of cake plates jostling in a pile allows us to postpone the inevitable a few minutes more as we arrange the contents on the table, dispense milk and sugar and search desperately for something else to fix upon. A reluctant cast in a farcical play, we concentrate fixedly on my mother's hands as cups are passed round.

"Granny, granny – look! I've found a bird's egg near the pond", squeals my nephew as he rushes into view, his sturdy six-year-old legs hurtling him into this fortress of disquiet. On a normal day, his delight would have been met with the promise of an investigation "after the adults have had a chat." Today, the interruption is welcome – provides a much-needed excuse to postpone the chat. Tension dissipates in a breath, replaced at once with the ease of familial gatherings, and collective relief.

We will talk later. Now is not the time. We can pretend for a few hours more. Until sunset, perhaps.

Michelle Burton

The Odd One Out

Jessie looked in the bathroom mirror and studied the face looking back at her. The pink ribbons stood out against her dark black curls. How she wished her hair was straight. She would brush it vigorously, hoping to pull the ringlets out, but she only succeeded in creating a frizzy mess that resembled wild, untamed straw. Her Mum often told her how beautiful her hair was, and would say that she wished her own hair was like Jessie's. Jessie did not think it beautiful at all and struggled to understand why her mum would want her hair. Her mother's hair was flat and blond, the comb sliding effortlessly through it. She did not battle against frizz or knots. And most importantly, her mother's hair looked like everyone else's.

It was Monday, the first day back to school after the summer holidays. Jessie had enjoyed a wonderful summer and wished it had not finished. She glanced down at her new uniform. It was crisp and perfect. She had been allowed to choose her own school skirt this time and took a long time deciding on the right one. It was a little mini skirt that flared slightly above the knee. Jessie had noticed the other girl's wore skirts like this. Perhaps she would blend in better with them now.

Jessie had to walk to school. It was only a few minutes away and part of the journey was pleasant. She liked walking along the path, breathing in the aroma of the brightly coloured plants. It was the acorn tree that ruined the walk. Once Jessie passed the tree the big roof of her school loomed, towering menacingly above the treetop. It was the spot Jessie hated more than anything.

Jessie heard her mother calling her from the kitchen. She made her way slowly down the stairs, desperately trying to avoid the inevitable. Her mother was stood at the bottom holding her shoes and coat.

"Quick Jess put them on. We don't want to be late," her mother said, kissing the top of her head. But Jessie did want to be late. In fact she had no desire to go at all.

They walked along the path in silence and Jessie tried walking with her eyes closed, hoping that she would miss the acorn tree. It didn't work. Jessie ended up stumbling over some stones and had to open her eyes again. Jessie knew that as soon as she got to the playground it would start. She might wear the same clothes, be the same height and even live in the same street, but Jessie would never be the same as everyone else. She was different to every child in her class. Her parents said it was because she was 'chosen.'

Jessie did not look like anybody she had met in real life. She was not even like her parents. They said it was what made her so special. They had picked her from the orphanage and chose her out of every other boy and girl there. But it wasn't just because of that. Jessie was different in another way too, and she longed more than anything to be exactly the same.

Once they reached the school gates, Jessie's mother kissed her goodbye. Jessie had another reason to feel apprehensive today. She was meeting her new class teacher that had come from another school across town. Thoughts raced through Jessie's mind. What if she didn't like Jessie? Jessie knew she stuck out like a sore thumb. Her heart pounded as she walked into the classroom and she heard giggling behind her. She hoped no one was laughing at her. Jessie walked over to her desk and sat down. As usual, no one was sat in the chair next to her. The children around her chattered loudly until the classroom door opened. A silence fell upon the class and the other children stared open mouthed. Jessie didn't, she smiled widely. The new teacher walked to the front of the class.

"Good morning class, I'm Miss Smith." She said in a friendly manner. Jessie wanted to hug her right there, for she was the same. Exactly the same. She had curly black hair too, but most importantly of all, she had the same coloured skin.

Gemma Middleton

The Swimming Pool Incident

The birthday girl

Oh God, I can't believe what I have done. Honestly, I'm not some crazed nutty person, it's just I... Look whatever I say I am going to sound like some sad, middle-aged woman. Do you know the saddest part of all this is that's exactly what I am? Today's my birthday, my 40th. I know I don't look a day over 39. Me and the girls had it all planned, it was going to be a night to remember and I don't mean sat here dripping on your floor. We were going to some real up-market nightclub. You know the sort; where you have to be over 15 and they serve your drinks in glasses. I had bought a whole new outfit from my shoes down to my underwear. But it was a flop from start to finish. The entertainment was going to be a stripper, they'd left that for Jane to organize, and you would have thought they would have known not to trust her, especially after that incident at the school fair with the cream cakes. Anyway, she was to ask for a Robbie Williams look-alike. What we got was a Robin Williams double. He definitely didn't have a six pack, more like two cans and a keg. He got to his belt and we asked him to stop, to be quite honest if I wanted to see things like that wobble, I could go back home.

Have you tried phoning my husband? He has been doing a lot of overtime recently; he never seems to be at home these days. I said to him the other day: "The amount of time you spend at that place, they'll be making you managing director." He gave me the look that said: "Someone has to earn the money to pay the credit card." That night he didn't get home till two in the morning. I guess he must have a key for the office and probably stayed there.

Anyway, back at the nightclub, I was getting so bored that even my teeth had fallen asleep. I couldn't even get drunk at £3 a glass and they were all umbrellas and vegetables, but at least I have had my five portions of fibre for the day! We started talking about the past. I remembered the massive crush I had on Johnny Tremble. I wanted to be one of his groupies but I couldn't afford the train fare and my mum wouldn't let me. He was so gorgeous. I was about 16 and he was 30, so mature and dangerous. I don't mean he would bite the heads off things but he had a special look and it felt as if all I needed to know was there in his eyes. God, he was sex on legs. Anyway, when Jane said she'd heard that he had moved in around here, I must confess I didn't really believe her. I thought it was more likely to be John Major, with her memory for names. Then a couple of the others piped up that she was right and that they had seen it on *Through the Keyhole* or something.

So that is where it all started, this was going to be my moment of rebellion, the something special for my birthday. We planned to go and just sort of look into the garden. See if we could see Johnny, nothing else. Once we got here the others started to lose enthusiasm, all of a sudden babysitters had to be relieved. Before I knew it I was on my own, looking at an empty garden and feeling so fed up and hot I thought I was going to melt. But I had come this far and I couldn't just go. So I decided to come in. I didn't break anything, just climbed over the fence. I was really surprised that no one stopped me. When I saw the swimming pool, I was so hot that it just seemed to be calling me in. I didn't have a costume and would have stayed in my underwear, but it is new. The bra is one of those that lifts and gives you a cleavage of a 20-year-old. It cost £30 and I was not going to risk the chlorine spoiling it. So that is why I was naked.

When Johnny came out, I really didn't recognise him, I thought it was his granddad. I guess none of us have aged that well. You know what it is like when you were a kid and you really wanted something for Christmas, then you get it and it is such a disappointment. That's what it was like seeing Johnny. He went such a strange colour when he started screaming, I thought he was going to have a heart attack. I honestly never planned any of this and I am really sorry. Oh my God, my moment of rebellion has gone horribly wrong. Can I go home now? I won't come near the house again. I think I had better get a taxi rather than bother my husband. He seems to get so angry with me these days.

Johnny Tremble
Where the bloody hell were you? What am I paying you to do for God's sake? Not to sit around on your arse and drink coffee. And what about that bloody mutt of yours? Where was it? Too busy licking its balls. That about sums up that Mickey Mouse company you work for. You aren't working for John Noakes. I am somebody. My claim to fame isn't two bog rolls and some sticky-backed plastic. I had women throwing more than just their pants at me. My groupies had groupies. Everywhere I went, people knew me. I even went on Parkinson once. How has it come to this, some sad, middle-aged fan swimming in my pool? Don't you know how careful we stars have to be with fans? She could have had a knife or a gun. What if the papers get to hear about it? Before I know it I could be in some sordid story in *The Sun*, "My Kinky Night of Passion with Johnny Tremble in His

Pool." And if it was the *Sunday Sport,* your dog would have been in there somewhere.

I was only going for a peaceful walk in the garden and I come face to face with some woman with all her bits out. She could have done anything. She could have tried to drug me. You know that date rape drug, retinal or Rennies, or whatever it's called. Then again I'm not sure it works on blokes. Are my golden dolphins OK, they cost me a bleeding fortune? I had them flown in from the States. The pool's got to be cleaned out. What was it with the naked bit? God, women really begin to sag as they get older, hit 35 and it all goes southwards, the whole lot begins to slide.

My third wife was one of my fans. We met at one of my gigs in the 1980s. I can tell you she didn't have any saggy bits, mind you she was about 10, or was it 15 years younger than me? Now she is screwing me for every penny she can get; alimony for an Afghan dog and Shetland pony, I wouldn't mind but I was the mug that bought them for her. Bachelor life is the way it is going to be from now on. Women will be a distant memory, in the case of my ex-wives, a nightmare. Don't get me wrong I haven't started batting for the other side or anything; I just need to concentrate on my future. The opposite sex has always been my downfall. Wife number two said I was a serial cheater. I told her that was Rock and Roll, if I was a banker I'd have to handle the money. Girls used to throw themselves at me and it would've been rude not to accept. Funny enough that didn't wash with her; mind you she did alright out of the settlement. She had enough money out of me to set up her own business. Last I heard she was one of the top ten wealthiest women.

Anyway my comeback is all set up. I have started writing a new album, it's going really well and

I can feel the old creative juices stirring. Song writing is an art and a craft that has to be worked at. Nowadays you can key two notes into a computer and you have a song. These man-made bands are fluff and foam. Kids today think that they can go on some crappy show and that's it, they've hit the big time. You've got to have more than white teeth and a good arse. Mind you my arse won a few awards in its time. God, I hope the shock of this won't cause a writer's block, things have been going great, I have written two songs. Well actually one and a half, but things are looking up. If Mick Jagger can keep going, then why not me? Singing is all I really know, I did dabble a bit in business but I made a few bad judgements and ended up losing a packet. What I have to work out is how to appeal to the younger market. Whether to go sexy like Tom Jones or cool like Elvis?

Did you get the woman's phone number? It's just, I've been thinking, a fan is a fan no matter what age she is and I could send her a copy of my new album when it's finished. Now I come to think of it she wasn't that bad looking after all and with clothes on, a good bra and a bit of make up, she could be quite attractive. I have slept with worse; I could call her just to see if things are OK. What do you reckon, did she seem like she might be up for it?

Alison Killeen

Colour of the Day

Esme stood before the wardrobe, humming absent-mindedly to herself. Glancing over at the window, she decided it was definitely a Purple day. While flicking through the scattered spectrum before her, she became aware of the music in her head and paused to identify it. Seconds passed, as she repeated the tune to herself, before a smile of recognition lit her face. "Muppets!" she laughed and continued with her search. Thirty minutes later, a vision in plum, Esme swept downstairs, smiled briefly at the mirror and paused to frown at her watch, before bursting unsuspectingly into the day.

Meanwhile, across town, Sophie Hillman sat in a coffee shop window, watching a man in a pinstripe suit trying to scrape dog shit off his expensive shoes. She watched as he repeatedly dragged his foot over the edge of the pavement opposite from her. He was trying desperately to maintain his dignity, but even at this distance she could see the crimson blush above his perfect Windsor knot. She stared openly at the unwitting clown, her lips tilting with amusement as she sipped her coffee, warming to its bitterness. Esme was late.

Sophie had known Esme all her life, from nappies to playground, through puberty to marriage. Sophie's marriage, that is: Esme had remained adamantly single. However, punctuality was fundamental to Sophie's personality and her friend's tardiness had been a source of unspoken annoyance for decades. Small slights piled upon vast betrayal. Sophie simmered quietly. Distracted by her thoughts, Sophie realised that Pinstripe had disappeared, leaving streaks of turd as evidence of the offence. Restlessly, she reapplied 'Iced Pink' to her lips, then neatly applied powder to her face, turning opalescence to chalk.

Esme breezed through the coffee shop doors, breathing in the heavy scent of fresh coffee, and the sweet smell of muffins. Spotting Sophie, she made her way towards her, pausing to watch her friend apply her cosmetic mask. She remained silent, smiling fondly at her friend's familiar ritual.

"You're late" said Sophie flatly, taking Esme by surprise and causing her smile to melt like brie on a hot summer's day. Sophie dropped the make-up into her bag, motioning Esme to sit.

"Who pissed in your cornflakes, honey?" Esme slumped into the seat opposite Sophie, disturbed by the frostiness exuding from her friend.

Sophie stared at her old friend. It was the same person, but how could it be? Now that Esme was here, Sophie felt scared to ask the question which had brought her here today. Everything in her carefully-controlled life had been turned upside-down at 9.36 the previous evening, but it would not become real until the words were said aloud. Looking into Esme's concerned eyes, she could picture them as girls, twirling and twirling, collapsing together in giggles on damp evening grass. The dry, awkward kisses derived from curiosity and patterned with laughter. Later, Esme as bridesmaid, looking incongruous in pink silk, smiling her on to the altar. Esme; vivacious and witty, charming Laurence with her comical story-telling and smiling brown eyes. She closed her eyes and pictured the red welts on her husband's back, glimpsed as he had stolen hastily into the shower upon his return from yet another 'business' trip. Breathing heavily, Sophie again smelt Esme's perfume, immediately recognised on Laurence's shirt as she tore through his clothes searching for clues.

"How long have you been fucking my husband?"

Of course she denied it all, cried and begged Sophie to believe in her innocence. Sophie had turned from her, fleeing the coffee shop, angry at Esme's deceit. As she rushed by taxi to the offices of Hillman and Jeffries, she planned how she would confront Laurence and to hell with who heard what she had to say. A little humiliation was the least he deserved.

Her mind ran in all directions, searching for answers, eventually settling on a day, years earlier, when Esme had confided her most recent sexual episode. How she had been carried away and drawn blood from scratches on her lover's back, and how awful she had felt when his shirt stuck to his skin. The entire tale told between fits of laughter. Tears of hurt and humiliation coursed lines through Sophie's foundation.

Sophie's legs felt unsteady as she stepped from the taxi, and she stopped to compose herself before entering the building. Her husband's assistant smiled flatly at Sophie: "Mrs Hillman, how nice to see you. I'll just call Laurie for you," she said, pressing a perfectly manicured finger onto the intercom button, "Your wife is here".

Laurence came swiftly out of his office, a puzzled look on his face as he walked toward her. A strange feeling came over Sophie, as Laurence said "Thank you, Sarah," and guided her into his office, past the sulky-looking assistant. He continued talking, something about time and shopping, but she felt as if she was reaching for something just out of her grasp. Laurence's voice had become distant. What was it?

"Why are you here, honey?"

Her mind suddenly caught up with what she already knew. The look that he had given *her*, almost a warning shot, as he had ushered Sophie through the door. Then, as she had passed his assistant, the smell of perfume.

Sophie did not make a scene but turned from Laurence and walked mutely out of the building, leaving a baffled husband calling after her.

It was a Black day.

Amanda Stone

The Wiccan Way

In a small, grubby office at Covent Garden market stood a short man in his mid-40s. He was stocky in build and had shoulder-length hair tied back with a rubber band. Sitting across the desk was an efficient-looking woman, her crisp suit making a stark contrast to his faded, crumpled jacket.

"It'll have to come down, Gary."

"What will? I'm sorry, you've lost me."

"The Halloween display, we've had complaints. The sooner the better." She returned her gaze to a pile of papers on her desk. This was her usual approach to dismissing staff but this time it wasn't successful.

"Who's complained?" Gary began to run his hand along his hair, down his thin pony tail. When he reached the end he began to twist it around his fingers. He was becoming irritated.

"Lots of people, Gary. It has made some feel quite uneasy." She hesitated and gave a weak smile adding: "Actually it's the Church, they're not happy. They feel the whole thing is far too Pagan. You know how they've been steering away from Hallowe'en. She'd had enough of this conversation and began to shuffle her papers.

"That's the whole point. It's a Pagan festival, not this American washed-out version. It was more about our history. It's…" The woman cut in before he could finish.

"Well, if you would like to tell that to the Archbishop's office, that's where the complaints have come from." She held up a curling fax. "Just take it down. I'm not taking on the Church of England." He knew that there was no point in arguing and left the office. He sighed. Just one more crap day to add to his crap week, which added to his crap life.

He went downstairs into the Apple Market and looked up at the metal arches which were swathed with red and black material. The black was transparent and the morning sun streamed through. This was to represent the veil between the two worlds that is supposed to be at its thinnest during Hallowe'en. Then there were the garlands of apples, pomegranates and plump baby pumpkins, which were twisted around the name sign. It had taken them days to wind wire around the fruits to make them into garlands. Gary had also hung Wicca symbols that represented the four elements; earth, air, fire and water. At the time he did wonder if maybe that was taking it a bit too far but he was determined for it to be a grown-up display - there would not be cartoon-shaped ghosts or witches on a broom stick. He had spent hours in the library researching it, just to make sure it was right.

"You OK, Gary?" Standing next to him was Bill, one of the market's maintenance men. He was shorter and rounder than Gary with hands covered in hard skin which had cracked and filled with dirt.

"Not really, Bill. All this has to come down." He nodded his head towards the arches.

"No! You're bleeding joking. All that sodding wire we used, it'll take us hours to get it down. What's wrong with it? "

"It's orders from her upstairs. The Church doesn't like it, so it has to go." Gary turned and looked at Bill who was now red in the face.

"Oh! Jesus Christ, Gary."

"Apparently he wasn't too keen on it either." The joke was lost on Bill as he walked away, grumbling under his breath. He went to get the platform to undo his hours of labour.

"Are you going tonight, Gary?" He turned to see Sally, a tall slender woman with hair that was long and wavy with thin strands of grey. As she smiled at him, he could see her bad teeth but there was warmth in her smile.

"Oh yeah, it's the Folk Club. Yeah, I'm going. Do you want a lift?"

"That would be great, if you don't mind." She walked back to her craft stall which was cluttered with an array of earrings and beads, all their colours jostling for attention.

Gary had joined the Folk Club a month back. Since his marriage break-up he needed things to try to fill his evenings, mainly to get out of his depressing bed-sit but also to take his mind off the dull ache that separation had caused. Things had started to go wrong after the birth of their second son. After their first son was born, they'd been told that because of the complications she wouldn't be able to have any more children. So when David came along they were both in their mid-40s. Looking back, Gary wasn't surprised that Ann had become depressed. What did shock him was that she blamed him. If the baby refused to sleep it was because Gary was banging doors. He either helped too much or he didn't help enough. One day she announced it was over, she wanted a divorce. He moved out into the bed-sit. That was five months ago and now he struggled to see his sons and every time they met it ended in a row. So he tried to fill his evenings with clubs and classes, anything but sit and stare at walls or start thinking.

That evening at the Folk Club he began to relax after a pint of beer. As the harmony of the music began to wash over him, he could put the day's events into context. So what if some Bishop didn't like his work? Next year he would stick to orange and black banners and pumpkins with faces cut out and candles in them. On the whole he enjoyed managing the Apple Market. It kept him busy and he liked working with people.

"You're miles away." Sally had come over and was now sitting down next to him.

"I've had a bit of a bad day. You know how it is," he sighed.

"Yeah, I couldn't believe that the display had to come down. I thought that it was really good, really authentic."

"Thanks. I just do as I'm told. I do the bidding for her upstairs."

"Do you want another drink?"

"No, I'm OK. Gary, I was wondering if you were in the craft. Do you belong to a coven?"

"Sorry?"

"Like I said your display was very authentic and so I was wondering if you were a Wiccan or a Pagan of some sort. Was I wrong?"

"Yeah, I just did a lot of research. Are you a…"

"A Wiccan, yes. I belong to the Docklands coven. Not an original name as we meet in the Docklands."

Gary had images of hairy dockers dancing around with a load of black-clad witches.

"Yes, where they've taken down some of the buildings, there's a stone circle. It's a bit derelict, not Stonehenge or Avebury, but it works well."

Gary was having a problem taking this in. He would never have thought that Sally was a witch. "Don't you get any problems? It seems such a public place."

"The occasional drunk likes to poke fun. Sorry to disappoint you but we don't run around in the nude. Well actually, sky-clad Wiccans do but it never really appealed to me. All those wobbly bits and candles just doesn't seem to be a good mix." This placed an unwanted image in Gary's head.

"There's a gathering tomorrow, why don't you come along?"

"Oh, I don't know. I'm not sure it is for me."

"Look, come along. You don't have to join the circle." Gary was intrigued. The research had stirred an interest and a lot of what he read seemed to make sense.

"OK, what time?"

When he picked Sally up the next evening, she was wearing a long purple dress with a plush green velvet cape over the top. As she moved, the fabric swished and her feet were hidden under the folds of material, giving the impression that she was floating. In the car she was very quiet and Gary didn't like to chat, he wasn't sure if she was preparing herself mentally.

As they drove towards Docklands, the surrounding areas became more run down. When they got to the place, there were mounds of rubble and discarded bits of building. The stone circle looked far from sacred. There were bits of old bricks sticking out of the ground. The circle itself was made up from four large blocks, set in a clumsy circle. In the centre was a small wooden table. Gary wasn't very sure how anything spiritual could be experienced here. He was warmly greeted by a number of the other members of the group, all of them dressed in robes similar to Sally's. Then everyone began to busy themselves. Someone had placed a cloth over the table and was now setting it with a small cauldron, red candles, a crystal ball and what he thought looked like a wand. Gary recognised an altar. Then onto the stones were placed different items. One had a bowl containing mud. Another had some incense placed on it. On the others were placed a large round candle and finally a bowl of water.

A hush fell over the group. A woman, dressed in a more elaborate gown than the others, walked to the four stones and placed burning incense onto each. She began with the stone covered with mud. Gary realised that she must be the High Priestess. Then, led by her, the group began to walk around the edge of the circle. The High Priestess held up a knife with a pearl white handle. Gary could just hear a gentle mumble coming from the group. It wasn't a shared chant; more a personal mantra. As they walked around they began gradually to speed up. Every now and then the High Priestess would point to one or other of the elements. As the pace began to step up, Gary could feel his head begin to swim: it was as if their movement was beginning to hypnotise him. He began to feel warmth from deep down inside. Their chants were getting louder. Gary thought that he was going to have to sit down because his head was spinning so much. The High Priestess dropped the knife; the blade glinted in the moonlight as it fell towards the ground. Then the chanting stopped and the High Priestess fell. As she hit the earth Gary felt a jolt go through his body. The thud broke him out of his daze and the next thing he knew he was eating cake and drinking strong, honey flavoured ale.

"Are you OK Gary?" Sally had come over with a plate of oat cakes.

"To be honest I feel a bit weird. The whole thing made me feel odd in the head and I got so hot. Is that normal, or am I sickening for something?"

"It's the power of the circle and it's even stronger the closer to the elements you get. That's where we get our energy. You obviously experienced something. I knew that you had the makings of a

Pagan." Just then the High Priestess came over. She was a large woman with powerful features.

"Hello, you must be Sally's friend. Did you enjoy the ceremony?"

Sally cut in before he could speak: "He felt the energy outside the circle. I can't remember anyone feeling anything from the outside, can you?"

"No. Gary, you are obviously very in tune to nature. Do you think you would like to join our group? You'd be most welcome.' She could see that he was a bit hesitant. "Sorry, I'm probably rushing you. Look, come to a couple more of our meetings and then you can decide if you want to be initiated."

She seemed genuinely pleased when Gary nodded.

"Next week we sacrifice a virgin." Gary's mouth dropped open and she laughed.

"Only joking, you'd be hard pushed to find one in London at this time of night." She walked off, still laughing.

It was then that Gary's life changed. His confidence grew and he felt less weighed down with his worries. He learned more about the Wiccan way of life. The chants they sang in the circle were spells used to protect their lives and that of others. When casting spells, Gary concentrated mainly on his two sons. He was still struggling to get regular access but he would avoid confrontation with Ann and tried to be as amicable as possible. He missed the boys with a pain that at times threatened to engulf him but transferring his inner energy to their protection seemed to help.

Things took a down turn one Monday morning. In the post came a large official-looking envelope. He opened it distractedly but the letter's content had his full attention. Ann was trying to stop him from having open access to the boys. He couldn't understand why, things had being getting better. He decided to phone her.

"I can't talk to you about it, Gary," she said. "Just come to the meeting."

"Yes, its next week, but I want to know what's going on."

'You'll find out then.'

On the day of the appointment Gary wore his best suit. He thought that if he looked smart it would give him more confidence but in fact it just made him feel awkward and uncomfortable. The solicitor's office was really upmarket and Gary couldn't work out how Ann could have afforded it. This definitely wasn't on legal aid. Just then Ann and Peter walked in.

"Hello, I didn't realise that you were bringing Peter. Isn't he a bit young to be involved in this?"

"He's 13, Gary, old enough to know his own mind. Anyway the solicitor said he needs to be here." As Gary looked at his son he could see Peter was uncomfortable with the situation. He gave his father a self-conscious smile and then looked down at his feet. His hands were stuffed in his coat pockets and his shoulders were hunched forward. Gary could feel anger rising inside. Didn't Peter have enough to cope with without adding to it? He desperately wanted to catch his attention, to give him a smile just to let him know it was going to be alright. But Peter kept his eyes fixed on the floor. The office was a large room with high ceilings, with bookcases around the walls. Mr Cove was sitting behind an impressive desk situated in a bay window.

"Right, I need to get you up to speed on what's going on. I don't know if you realise but I'm actually a governmental solicitor. I've been brought in on your access case because there are some concerns about your links to witchcraft."

"What!?"

"It's felt things need to be more closely looked at because you're a witch." The solicitor picked up his pen and began to roll it between his fingers.

"What've my beliefs got to do with what sort of father I am?"

"Your beliefs aren't exactly mainstream and there are concerns for the children's welfare." Gary could feel the anger rising in him. What right did this pompous prick have to tell him how to look after his children?

"Paganism has been around for years, even before Christianity. So you can't say it's not mainstream."

"What we mean is it's not practised by many people these days. And those that do, tend to have alternative life styles."

Gary couldn't believe what he was hearing.

"So would you say that university lecturers, teachers, shop managers and an Inland Revenue inspector, who I believe is also employed by the government, aren't mainstream. I know people in all those professions that are Wiccans. And some of them have children that are healthy and happy." Gary was now sitting on the edge of his chair, trying to stop himself getting up and banging the desk.

"That may be, but we are concerned with the welfare of your two sons."

"And how can you stopping me from seeing them be good for their welfare?"

"Mr Rimes, we aren't talking about stopping your access, just having your visits supervised."

"So, I'll have someone watching me all the time I am with the boys?"

"Well, yes. We don't want the boys exposed to anything inappropriate. There is a sexual element to your beliefs isn't there?"

"Yes, but I wouldn't take the boys to a ceremony. Firstly they are too young, you have to be 16, and secondly they wouldn't be allowed to attend because they aren't initiated. So, if I promise not to take them to any ceremonies can I have open access?"

"It's not as simple as that. We don't want you talking to the boys about your beliefs."

"What! So I can't talk to them either?"

Then all of a sudden Peter shouted out: "That's rubbish!"

For a minute Mr Cove looked taken aback but then he turned to Peter and said: "Would you like to say something?"

"You not letting Dad talk about being a Wiccan is rubbish. I could go to libraries or bookshops and get loads of books on it? And you can get books on spells and stuff as well. Wouldn't it be better for me to find out about it from Dad and not some stupid book?"

This was the most Gary had heard Peter say for years. He could feel tear stinging the backs of his eyes as his son defended him.

"You've a point there. Is being a Wiccan something that interests you?" Mr Cove was sitting forward and was resting his arms on his desk.

"No, but if it did I'd rather go to my Dad to find out about it."

Mr Cove looked at Peter for some time, as if digesting what had been said.

"I think this boy has made a valid point. Therefore, with that in mind, I don't feel there should be any changes to your access." Gary leaped out of his chair and threw his arms around his son. Peter flinched initially but then returned the hug.

Twelve years on and Gary still has close contact with his sons. Peter is now grown but still sees his father regularly and they spend a large part of the school holidays together. Neither boy has followed his father into witchcraft. Gary moved away from London and now lives in Avebury in Wiltshire. He and his new partner, Natasha, have set up home in a small cottage within walking distance of the stone circles. They are both practising Wiccans and Gary is now a High Priest of The Woodlands Coven. They are a small group of about seven members who worship within the ancient circles. There has also been a dramatic change in Gary's career. He now works as an odd-job man, helps at an organic chicken farm, is a street performer and sometimes performs at corporate events. He also describes himself, with a laugh in his voice, as a house-husband. Natasha is his junior by about 20 years and works as a Marketing manager for NTL.

Gary lives his life close to nature and runs it on the path of the moon. He will only plant seeds at a particular time of the month, planting them at the darkest day because that time is followed soon by a strong full moon. His life style may seem sedentary compared to his early years but he has a real inner peace. It is hard to tell whether Gary's peace is due to living life in the Wiccan way or just finding the right path for him. But he does seem a contented man.

Alison Killeen

Enjoying the Ride

The lights surrounded him, vivid, alive, engulfing him in the beauty. He listened to the music as his carriage whizzed past the loudspeakers, throwing his body from side to side. He felt his face tingling in the cold night air as he spun round. Next, he rode the Big Wheel. From above he could see everything. He was sure he saw his father down there, holding his mother's hand. He thought that strange, but could not think why. He noticed he was riding solo again and also thought that peculiar. Again, he did not know why. What happened next puzzled him. He was sitting on a carousel, up, down, his stomach lurching occasionally. He could see all the other brightly coloured horses raising and lowering, but they had no riders. He looked out into the crowd again, recognizing faces from a time long ago, feeling safe, but unsure. The smell of candyfloss. He knew he loved the fair but felt like he didn't belong. People in the crowds started waving, their faces blurring as he whirled around them on his bright horse. He felt the ride get faster, out of control. He saw a big light raise from the middle of the carousel and he thought his eyes were playing tricks on him, as they often had in his later years. Then he began to remember and felt scared.

"We have lost him," the doctor said, looking at his companions. "Time of death, 12.37"

Gemma Middleton

The Amanda Show

<u>February</u>
It's the latest episode of the long-running reality show imaginatively titled '*The Amanda Show*'. The star of the show is sitting at her dining table, eating a wonderfully healthy meal of tomatoes, peppers, coleslaw, lettuce, cucumber, beetroot and couscous. The room is immaculate and she is a picture of joyful domesticity. Her loyal audience, having watched Amanda first clean the bathroom (even behind the loo), then vacuum throughout the house, followed by the wiping of the kitchen cupboard doors and concluding with the emptying of the wastepaper bins, are sure to agree that a break is well deserved. As she sits peacefully at the table, they think she is perhaps planning a delicious dinner for James, her beloved husband, or compiling a shopping list in her head.
(Amanda sips water).

Or maybe she is trying to decide whether to clean the oven or if alphabetising the contents of the kitchen cupboards is, in fact, more of a priority.

Amanda is thinking that a pathologist, emptying out her stomach contents could well be forgiven for believing her to be a healthy eater, which belies her slightly plump appearance.
(Amanda blots her lips with a napkin).

The audience watch as Amanda places the plate in the dish washer and then returns to the dining room, heading toward the dust-free stereo. She pushes a couple of buttons and Joni Mitchell begins to serenade suburbia. Amanda briefly disappears from sight as she answers a call of nature. The viewers take this opportunity to quickly pop to the kitchen to make a cup of tea.

Amanda speculates as to whether she is being watched having a piss, and makes sure to wash her hands thoroughly with the antibacterial soap.

Now the audience watch as Amanda sorts the laundry (red wash, white wash, dark wash, towels). Thousands are soothed by the familiarity of her routine, an image to hold onto and a vicarious comforter for those suffering the highs and lows of real life. As Amanda loads the washing into the machine, the viewers know that this is how life really should be, if only they were not so busy living it.
(Amanda hums along with Ms Mitchell, whilst adding detergent and fabric conditioner).

Amanda doubts that Joni has to wash skid marks out of anybody's boxers.

Later that day, the audience switch on the TV, ready to watch Amanda doing the grocery shop. It is Thursday, and a definite highlight of the week, always full of surprises. Bacon - smoked or unsmoked? Granny Smith or Braeburn this week? Will she remember to buy mangetout instead of sugar snap? James really was not happy about that little fiasco.
(Amanda enters the vegetable section).

Mangetout. What a relief. She looks around her. The audience are transfixed; maybe she is going to risk some baby corn or those cute miniature cauliflowers. No, she does not picked up anything else in the vegetable section. Disappointment leads to many switching channels, while the more loyal followers settle for either a bathroom or refreshment break.

Amanda's quick glance around has led her to wonder what's going on with the wardrobe department. The extras are looking far too dishevelled. After all, there's realism and then there's just plain silly.

That night. Amanda is lying in bed, James sleeps heavily beside her. There is increasing concern over Amanda's insomnia. Many believe that she should switch to decaf; surely she knows that caffeine is a real no-no. Letters have been sent, asking the show's producers to intervene. It has been suggested that they should even go so far as to substitute the contents of the jars on the supermarket shelves.

In contrast, the producers are simply relieved that Amanda has stopped initiating sex, as poor James was contractually obliged to respond. They had lost so many night viewers, due to them having to switch to landscape views and Vivaldi during earlier series of the show.
(Amanda's eyes flicker, then snap open).

Oh God, thinks Amanda, what if I snore? Or worse, fart! Stay awake for Christ's sake, woman.

The ratings reveal that most viewers gave up and switched off, long before Amanda fell asleep. This is happening more and more, as the public comes to realise that Amanda will simply lie there and, guess as they might (because they know her so well), they just can't seem to work out what she is thinking. Ennui eventually defeats both curiosity and loyalty.

March

Manicure on third Tuesday of the month. Thursday afternoons in Waitrose. Weight loss, 2lbs. Hair colour changed from 'Rich Mahogany' to 'Deeply Chestnut', not that James noticed. Ratings wane slightly. Producers have emergency meetings. No landscapes or Vivaldi.

April

Ratings peak, as concerned public tune back in, after particularly dramatic episode, shows Amanda being prescribed Prozac: Headlines such as 'Amanda

Turns to Drugs', appear on magazine racks. During a visit to the UK, Hollywood star, Tom Cruise slates 'The Amanda Show', saying that such a publicity stunt risks more people being deluded into believing that depression is a genuine illness. Lack of landscapes and Vivaldi are blamed for Amanda's unfortunate condition.

May

Amanda is seated at her dining room table. She appears lost in thought, and her salad has begun to curl and brown in front of her. The bathroom has been cleaned, along with the kitchen, lounge and dining room. She has been singing along with Eva Cassidy for most of the morning. Things are once more as they should be. Viewers' feelings of shock are beginning to fade as Amanda returns to being the perfect wife they love. A blind eye is nationally turned to the little pills that she now takes along with her daily vitamins. Few consider what could be going on behind her neat façade. Surely it is, after all, safer to go by appearances.
(Amanda looks down at her rapidly wilting lunch).

Pizza, I just want pizza. The mantra plays on repeat in her head.

The slightly concerned viewers watch as Amanda scrapes her lunch into the bin. They are calmed by the fact that she then carefully places the redundant kitchenware in the correct parts of the dishwasher. Ok, they reassure themselves, so she simply wasn't hungry.

It's Thursday, and Amanda sets of to the supermarket with her carefully scribed shopping list. Oh dear, sugarsnaps. James will not be pleased. What's that? Golden Delicious! She's picked up the wrong bag; she must have mistaken them for Granny

Smith's. Gasp! Panic-stricken viewers across the nation.

In the wines and alcoholic beverages aisle, an unpleasant woman of about 40 (but dressed like a woman half her age), pushes Amanda out of the way in order to get the last bottle of James's favourite frascati. The audience are rapt as Amanda simply turns toward this stranger, smiling ever so sweetly, and asks the woman if she can recommend a good chardonnay. As mystified viewers look on, the woman grunts and replies: "That Blossom Hill stuff is pretty good." Thanking her politely, Amanda inexplicably picks the suggested wine from the shelf and adds it to her shopping.

What on Earth is going on? James would never drink that. Amanda is making so many errors today that some members of the public begin mutinously to believe that she is purposely getting things wrong.

(Amanda heads towards the organic section).

I really do prefer red wine, thinks Amanda. Her angelic smile twitches slightly as she secretly hopes the woman will get fired. Extras, remember, are not supposed to speak.

June

Towards the end of the month, viewers tuning into the midmorning airing of 'The Amanda Show', are surprised to find themselves presented with a slideshow of pictures depicting Amanda washing-up, Amanda making the beds, Amanda doing her make-up etc, accompanied by a soundtrack of bird song. (Vivaldi and the landscapes having been long retired from the show, emergency action has inspired the production team into producing an Amanda montage, along with a recording left in the studio by a nature programme.)

Members of the show's audience slowly put two and two together. James must be home they surmise. Perhaps the pitter-patter of tiny feet will soon be joining the show after all.
(End birdsong, cue live action).

Amanda is doing her hair in front of the hall mirror. Where's James? Puzzled viewers decide that he has either returned to work, or there has been a technical fault. Any other possibilities are swiftly pushed from viewers' minds. This is 'The Amanda Show' they remind themselves.

Amanda smiles at her reflection. Wow, James is so wrong when he says that women can't do DIY.

Thursday. Amanda accomplishes her shop perfectly, even securing a few extra bottles of James's favourite tipple.

He's going to need these, muses Amanda, as she adds a couple more to the trolley.

The audience watch in surprise as she heads towards the cash-point machine. Cash withdrawals on a Thursday, since when? Her 'pin-money' is always withdrawn on a Monday. As ever, the area containing the screen is blurred for security's sake, and the frustrated viewers are left to guess how much Amanda has secreted in her purse.

That night, the Amanda montage is once more to be seen with accompanying birdsong (landscapes and Vivaldi having been permanently retired, following a landslide victory in viewer response surveys for the new-style interlude). A contented audience looks forward to the announcement of a future blessed event.

The following day, James has left for work and Amanda is sitting in the lounge drinking coffee (still not decaffeinated, note viewers; that will certainly have to change soon). She finishes her drink and rises, ready for the day's work ahead.

(Amanda enters bedroom).

The audience are captivated as she begins to empty her clothes out of the wardrobe, onto the bed. Oh goody, she's having a clearout. Viewers settle down to see what Amanda selects for the charity shop this time, eagerly anticipating the inevitable shopping trip to follow.

By the time that Amanda has finished packing her cases, both the show's producers and the viewing public are deep in a state of denial.

(Amanda looks round the kitchen).

She has placed a brief note on the counter, next to the frascati, explaining how extra portions of meals that she has been preparing over the last month are each carefully labelled in the bottom two drawers of the freezer.

No point in waiting to say any goodbyes, considers Amanda. After all, James probably won't even notice until his dinner does not arrive. Clothes, money, pills, make-up, car keys...she runs through the list in her mind as she stands in the hallway. The car is loaded, and it is time to make her final exit.

The audience in mourning are left helpless to watch as Amanda walks out the door. The camera pans around the sterile room. She is gone.

*As Amanda locks the door, she consciously leaves behind the 'show' that she has been living. She feels a slight thrill of fear at leaving behind the fantasy that has kept her going for so long, the force that had gotten her out of bed and that had enabled her to perform that which she would otherwise have been unable to perform for the husband that she now realises had not really married **her.***

(Amanda backs out of drive).

Permitting herself one final flight-of-fancy, she imagines the power surge that would result from televisions being switched on as word gets out that

'The Amanda Show' has finally become interesting. She laughs lightly as she leaves the show behind for her biggest shopping trip ever - to get a life.

Amanda Stone

It Is Worse

It is worse. Much worse. It is worse than you ever expected it would be. More painful, too. And deeper in its wounding than you thought it had depth to go. It is harder to bear than the loss of a friend. It is more powerful to withstand than the angry elements of a thundered storm. It is more dangerous to your soul than emptiness or lack or despair. It is worse than the first time love left your heart in a thousand youthful shards. It is worse – much, much worse: The day your son says he hates you.

Michelle Burton

Settee

I was once a deep red but my colour has faded. If you look into my creases you can see how I used to be. My cushions are flat and saggy where they used to be firm and pert; waiting to give comfort. On my arms there are sticky patches, the remains of some discarded sweets. My covers drag on the floor and the buttons at the back don't quite do up. Time has taken its toll. I have seen so much and remember every little detail. I remember the cats which started off as playful kittens chasing around my hems. We shared many a sunny afternoon as they purred and left small beads of dribble on my covers. Then their slow, lumbering movement as they grow old, until one day I didn't see them any more. But deep down behind my cushions, hidden away, I have kept some of their hairs.

So many changes. I remember the fumbling passion of the parents that led to the children. They would start off so small, leaving puddles and milky sick. Then as they got older, I became part of their games; I would be a boat on the high seas or a den in which to hide and keep the big bad wolf at bay. Now their puppy fat has turned into muscular adolescence covered in prickly hair and spots. They lie languidly across me, their apathy seeping down to my springs.

Once I had a passion. I longed to be a chaise lounge, with elegant curves. I wanted to smell of French perfume, with frills that skirted just above my shapely wooden legs. But now that dream has faded, along with my colour. They pile catalogues of modern furniture on me. I know it won't be long before I am replaced with a chocolate brown leather settee with contrasting cushions. I don't really mind.

I am tired and have given good service over the years and it will be good to see the cats again.

Alison Killeen

Picture Perfect

He looked down into the warm brown eyes that shone up at him. Simoriah. He stroked his fingers lovingly along her jaw, then gently tilted her chin and rested the lightest of kisses on the tip of her nose. "Drink up, sweetheart. Time for sleep."

"Yes Daddy, I love you." She held her drink tightly in both hands, swallowing the remaining cordial in one enthusiastic gulp.

He watched as she lay down between two of her sisters, her lips still curled into a dreamy smile as her eyelids softly closed. The room was still, and from outside the window he could hear birds singing a twilight lullaby. It was perfect. A strong surge of pride engulfed him as he looked down at the sleeping angels before him.

"Look at the picture!"

He smiled indulgently at the fool sat across from him, and slowly leant forward to look at the picture. "Ah, Selene, Simoriah and Demelza. They look beautiful, don't they?"

A thick, nicotine-stained finger pointed to each of the girls. "Ruth Peterson, 22; Sarah-Jane Grant, 24; and Heather Jones, just 18." Inspector John Hunt continued, keeping his voice even: "They look dead."

The prisoner sat back in the hard plastic chair, his smile remaining fixed as he stroked his thick blonde hair into place; his eyes never leaving those of the Inspector. He already knew that the guy was left-handed, a smoker and possibly either divorced or separated, although he hoped the removal of his wedding ring had been for his benefit. Fear is flattering. There were two guards posted outside the door and, no doubt, several officers watching the interview from the next room. The door was approximately eight feet away in a two o'clock position. Hunt was a mere three feet away. Impressed by his observations of the situation, Robert "Daddy" Hudson felt relaxed and was looking forward to playing out the game.

Amanda Stone

Chocolate Chip Muffin

She looked down at the scales and saw the needle fluttering just above the half-way mark. She stepped off and removed her bra and pants, she then stood back on. The needle was now under the half. She felt jubilant; four pounds lost in one week. This was cause for a celebration. Usually her treat would be a bar of chocolate, or a piece of cake but that was out of the question. Her next favourite thing was to go into town and to try on clothes that were too large for her. She loved to feel the waist band sliding to her hips. It was a strange ritual but helped to boost her ego.

Walking into town she held her head high and tried to catch a glimpse of her reflection in shop windows. She felt sure that she looked trimmer. Then her stomach let out a grumbling moan. In her haste to get to the shops she had forgotten to have breakfast. This was the most important meal of the day, according to all the magazines, and she really ought to get something to eat. The smell of coffee caught her as and she decided that she would see what was on offer to eat. As she walked into the café, the coffee smell was really powerful, mixing with the sweet scent of cakes and biscuits. Then she saw it. It was sat in a paper case; its edges spilled over the top and hung like a roll of fat over a waste band. Its top was encrusted with large, glistening chunks of chocolate. This was a muffin of perfection. She could feel the saliva begin to fill her mouth but she couldn't have it. The muffin alone would take up half her daily calorie allowance. No, she had to make a sensible choice. A bread roll and a coffee would do the job. That was it, that's what to have.

"Could I have a skinny Latté and a bread roll?' The girl busied herself with the coffee machine. Out of the corner of her eye she could see the muffin; the chocolate had begun to sweat under the lights and the yellow of the sponge seemed florescent next to it. She could feel her mouth begin to water again. This was ludicrous. It was just a cake, she thought, a cake that she couldn't have. Just then the girl returned with her coffee.

'One skinny Latté, what else was it?'

'Hum…, a chocolate chip muffin,' she said quickly in a low, guilty voice. Oh well, if she skipped lunch and then had a salad for tea that would make up for it.

Alison Killeen

Worth the Risk

His heart pounded, the perspiration vivid along his brow. He knew that his hand would have to be placed into that big void if he was to retrieve the hidden treasure.

Gingerly, he touched the top of whatever substance distanced him and the life-changing object that lay beneath. He envisioned the monster that would be waiting, desperate to taste the fresh blood of his young fingers. He shut his eyes as his hand went deeper. Moving his fingers gently, he rummaged for the gift, scraping and feeling for anything that would make this experience worthwhile. And then…he felt something. Using all the strength a seven-year-old could muster, he withdrew his prize from the Lucky Dip box.

Gemma Middleton

The Frog Prince

Having spent a busy morning doing charity work, a spread on *Fashion for the Homeless*, Camilla Posh-Toff decided to reward herself with a well-earned facial followed by a few drinks with the 'girls' at her favourite bar. The paparazzi would unfortunately be out in full force, but how can a girl avoid them and still get a decent glass of champagne?

At 25 years of age, Camilla was the most popular 'It-Girl' in town. She had become known as 'The Tabloid Princess', a name which she detested. Despite her dismay, she was gracious enough to answer to it, and had actually called her little restaurant by the same name, purely as a joke, obviously. Single and stunning, though perhaps just a little goggle-eyed, Camilla had a stream of rich and successful admirers. Her over-wide mouth was never commented on and could be easily overlooked as her pedigree was so perfect. This also allowed her slightly-webbed toes to go unnoticed in her Jimmy Choo's.

As she left her apartment building, passing the pool and fountain in the ground floor lobby, she stopped to look at her reflection in a mirror which had been carefully placed behind the streams of water. This was her favourite place to admire herself, surrounded by sparkling reflected light which resulted in a far kinder image than most mirrors. Leaning over the edge of the deep pool, Camilla lost grip of her handbag (absolutely the latest design, made of reconstituted terry nappies and razor blades which had been carefully blunted by lots of lovely little Asian children in those sweet shops they are always on about). Highly distressed, almost to the point of mascara run, she stamped her foot and wailed for her lost bag (not to mention the little blue pills inside).

Drawn by the flow of the water, the bag moved until it was out of reach and then proceeded to sink. Looking at her perfectly manicured hands and designer-clad body, Camilla rejected any idea of attempting to salvage the bag herself.

She was toying with whether the Fire Brigade would recognise the magnitude of such an emergency, when suddenly a strange voice from somewhere nearby said: "Don't cry, honey. I'll get it back if you'll do me just one favour." Looking around, Camilla located the owner of the voice, a strange little frog sitting on the side of the pool. Surprised and more than a little repulsed, Camilla could not help being intrigued by his offer.

"Where did you come from?" gasped Camilla, edging away from the slimy amphibian. "Around," the frog answered evasively. "What do you say? Do you want to make a deal?" Camilla was sceptical about the creature being able to help but seeing no other assistance, let out a derisive snort and asked bluntly: "What favour?"

The frog ignored her rudeness: "All I ask in return for retrieving your bag is that you allow me to live with you as your companion, sharing your meals, sleeping beside you and kissing you goodnight."

Camilla shuddered at the thought of sharing her carefully-measured salads with the creature and felt positively nauseous at the suggestion that she should allow the slimy fellow to lie on her silken sheets. As for kissing the beastly thing it was quite out of the question. Fighting to conceal her aversion to the frog, she smiled her favourite Hello Cover Smile and said: "That sounds perfectly fine to me, but pleases hurry before it starts to rust."

In an instant, the frog was in the water, and with a strength that seemed incongruous for such a small individual, he recovered the £2,000 fashion must-have of the month, returning it to Camilla's outstretched hands.

Camilla shrieked with delight, holding the dripping bag at arms' reach. She then poked her tongue out at the expectant rescuer and ran laughing towards the exit. The deceived champion was left to hop along in her wake, calling after her: "Wait sweet Camilla, I can't keep up!" The door swung back towards him, hitting him full-on, and projecting him across the lobby floor, to land in a heap of slimy legs and bewilderment.

"Bitch!" croaked the hero.

Amanda Stone

After…

An eight-year-old girl sits on her chair, her knees up to her chest and her arms tightly clasped around her legs. She gives off a casual air but her eyes are moving rapidly from side to side. She is taking in all that is happening around her in the class room. The room is full of the sounds of other children enjoying their afternoon. They pay little attention to the girl on the chair; they have long since given up trying to get her to join in. Her chair gets a wide birth as once too often have they caught a blow from her hand.

The teacher looks over. She also ignores the fact that the girl is not taking part, after spending many hours trying to get her to join in. None of the strategies she had been taught at teacher training college has helped. The girl just stares with her unsmiling eyes. There were times when the girl used to shout out streams of foul language or throw her books across the table. So it was better for the other children if she just sat there.

The teacher feels out of her depth. She remembered the way the girl was before, an able student who worked hard. Once she was a popular girl, playing like the other children and smiling. The teacher sighs and moved over to a group of children squabbling over a pot of glue.

The girl's mother stands by the window and waits to pick her up from school, counting the hours until her daughter will be back. The girl's mother did once have a job working in the local supermarket. She would spend time chatting to the customers and enjoying their company. Now she stands and waits. She twists her wedding ring around and pulls it up to her knuckle and then pushes it back down. She can no longer do her job in the supermarket as she needs to be able to stand and wait. It wasn't like this before. Then she would have rushed from work to be able to meet the girl from school. She would stand outside trying to catch her breath and wait for the girl's smiling face to appear, arms laden with lunch box and book bag and her cardigan dragging on the floor. Laughing, she handed it all over to her mother.

The mother sighed and moved away from the window. She would go upstairs and check the girl's room to make sure that the covers on the bed were straight. Then she would stand and take in the peace and soak up the memories. She would take a teddy, hold it to her nose and breathe in, trying to catch the girl's scent. But there was no trace. The girl no longer slept with her teddy bears.

The girl's father works in a busy office. All around him is the noise of the phones ringing, people talking and laughing. He likes to keep working until he is so tired that his eyes threaten to close when he drives home. He fills his days and evenings with the constant hum of his computer and phones unknown people in distant places. There is always more work that needs to be done and his working week begins to drift into the weekends. Before, he would leave his office at 6 and be back home at 6.30. The girl ran to him as he walked through the front door. She would tell him all about her day in a rush of sentences, stopping briefly mid-flow to kiss him then carry on. He would lie on her bed and read her *Harry Potter*. When they came to a scary bit she would twist her fingers into his and beg for him to carry on reading when it was time for bed.

Now he doesn't get in until she is asleep so as to avoid her dark brown eyes. Neither does he have to see his wife watching their daughter, rigid with anxiety. He knows he is too weak to help. As a phone rings he is taken back to his office world, a place where every thing is the same as before.

The girl's older sister sits in a toilet cubical. The door is locked and she searches for a well-hidden pin. Then she drags it across her arm, a red welt appears. On the third scrape, a droplet of red blood springs to her skin. Then she feels the relief, the warm comfort that helps to take away the sick pain that is deep in her stomach. At that moment nothing else matters but the feeling of comfort and the red. Before, her little sister would pester her to play her games, watch films and to go out shopping. Though the eyes still follow her around the room, the girl doesn't pester anymore. The sister sometimes offers to paint the girl's nails but the girl only shakes her head.

The girl's mother remembers the day, replaying each second of it in slow motion just to see if there was something that she could have done. The girl went to play out front; nothing unusual in this. As the mother did her housework she would check from a window to make sure that she could still see the girl skipping up the street or flying past on her bike. Occasionally the girl would stop to push a long strand of her hair behind her ear or to pull up a crumpled sock. Later as the mother pushed the Hoover around she felt her stomach grumble, looked at the clock and saw it was past their lunchtime. She turned off the Hoover and went to call the girl in for lunch. As she stood at the front door she couldn't see her, so she moved down to the gate to give her a clear view of the road. The mother began to feel irritation rise, the girl must have wandered off. Maybe she had gone to her friend's house; why didn't she come and ask her? When she got to the house, no one had seen the girl all day. Then the panic took over. The girl's mother began to walk down the street calling her name. She banged on her neighbours' doors. The street began to fill with neighbours all looking for the girl, calling out her name. Maybe there was a homemade den that might have drawn her? Each location was searched but to no avail. Then someone said that they should call the police. They turned up in cars filling the street with their white and blue.

When was the last time she saw the girl? What was she wearing? Had there been a row? The girl's mother struggled to think of the answers. Two hours ago, or was it three? She thought she was wearing pink shorts but they might have been purple and, no, there was no row. Why were they asking all these questions and not out looking for her daughter?

As time passed, the mother's dumb hope that the girl would walk up the street began to fade. Nevertheless the girl's mother stood in front of the sitting room window and waited. She refused to eat and sleep but took small sips of water out of plastic cups that the policewoman gave her. She kept up her tireless vigil, hardly moving from the window. Two days later they found her in a bed-sit on the other side of town; that was all the police would say. The girl's mother dared not believe it until she held her in her arms. When the girl's mother saw her, she felt a sudden burst of joy and exhaustion, realising just how long she had been standing and how tired her legs felt. She fell to her knees as she wrapped her arms around her daughter. Different and strange smells came off her hair and she realised that the girl wasn't hugging back. The girl's mother began to sob, quietly at first, then they turned into silent screams and then into howls that spread through the house. She had lost her little girl and nothing would be like it was before.

The girl's father remembers it was 3 o'clock when he got the phone call as he couldn't understand why his wife hadn't phoned him herself. When he got back to his home he was surprised by the number of people in the street, all searching and calling out the girl's name. Inside the house seemed just as full as the street; there were a couple of police officers. Then he saw his wife and tried to talk to her but she seemed not to hear him, just kept staring straight ahead. The girl's father knew that he couldn't stay and wait, he had to be out doing something. He began his search in places that had been gone over 10 times before but he had to be sure that they had been checked properly. He walked and walked until his legs were heavy. Only then would he return home to eat dry, tasteless sandwiches and catch a couple of hours' sleep. As soon as it was light again he would return to his searching. When he got the phone call saying that she had been found he couldn't believe it, not till he had seen her and touched her. When he stepped through the door he heard his wife's cries. He had a sick feeling deep in his stomach and thought they must have got it wrong. But then he saw his little girl, his wife was kneeling in front of her. His wife was screaming and trails of mucus ran from her nose. He couldn't understand what was wrong or why his wife was behaving like this. Then he saw her eyes, looking at him and blaming him for not being there, not keeping her safe. Then he was too scared to touch her or hold her.

The thing he fears most is that he will never be able to wrap his arms around her again. Pick her up, inches from the ground and swing her around as she squeals with delight. Never again feel her nuzzle her face into his neck and tell him that she loves him.

The girl's sister knows that it is all her fault what happened that day. She could have stopped it from happening if she hadn't been so selfish. The girl had begged to come into town but her sister didn't want her dragging round after them. She knew that she would smile at their jokes when she really couldn't understand them and ask stupid questions. As she got nearer the house she saw the police cars and felt a sick pain deep in her stomach. Inside, the house was full of people who all seemed to be ignoring her, avoiding her eyes. She went over to her mother to find out what had happened. But she didn't see her either; all she was doing was staring out of the window. She remembers the feel of the policewoman's hand on her arm as she said that everyone was doing what they could. She had to do something to help. So she began to make endless cups of tea for everyone, everyone except her mother. When her father came home he folded his arms around her and held her tight. Before she could say anything he was out of the house, hunting for her sister. Hours and loads of cups of tea later the phone call came. No one told her what was happening but she saw them bring her little sister in. It was then her mother began to cry, so loudly and snot ran down her mother's face which was embarrassing, so she went back to the kitchen and cried quietly on her own.

The man sits in his cell and waits. He spends his time reading, doing crosswords and waiting for the time to pass. He will pay his debt to society and go to all the meetings, repent his wrong ways and then wait. He will wait until they can see that he has become that model citizen they want and then, after that…He will watch from afar. A smile flutters across the man's face and he returns his gaze to his crossword. He has all the time in the world.

Alison Killeen

Extract from the un-published novel 'Hiding'

CHAPTER 1

Jasmine threw back the covers and sighed. The neon green light of the clock flashed the time at her: 3.10 AM. She had been awake for hours and it would soon be time to get up. Jasmine closed her eyes and tried to snuggle closer into Marie, who was lucky enough to be asleep. Marie shrugged her arm and pulled the duvet up around her body, cocooning herself from Jasmine's touch. Jasmine both loved and loathed Marie's ability to sleep no matter what was happening. In fact, the more Jasmine thought about it, she loved and loathed a lot of things about Marie. As sleep would not come, Jasmine allowed her brain a free rein. She had an awful lot to think about.

The alarm startled her. She had dozed off at some point and now she felt terrible. The room was still dark, the heavy drapes keeping out any sun that might be greeting the rest of the world. Jasmine turned over, suddenly aware of an empty space next to her. Another annoying attribute Marie possessed: a built-in alarm clock that woke her every morning at 6.30. While Jasmine often struggled to gain consciousness, Marie would jump out of bed and start her daily routine. As it was now gone 7, Jasmine knew Marie would be in the shower with a fresh pot of coffee ready downstairs in the kitchen. With a heavy head and an awful taste in her mouth, Jasmine pulled herself out of bed and stood up.

"Good morning, beautiful," said Marie, her eyes alert and studying Jasmine intently. She was stood at the kitchen unit buttering toast, still wrapped in a towel and smelling of the lavender shower gel she always used. Jasmine inhaled both Marie and the coffee. She didn't answer but walked up behind her and kissed her softly on the neck. A black cup of coffee sat waiting for Jasmine next to the toaster and she picked it up.

"Thanks."

Jasmine took a huge gulp and relished the caffeine hit to her brain. The sun streamed through the kitchen window, indicating a warm day ahead. Marie took her toast and sat down at the table. Jasmine walked over and joined her. Jasmine loved this kitchen; it was her favourite room in the house. She always felt relaxed here and had often joked to Marie that she should put her bed here to get a good night's sleep. The yellow hues of the walls made her feel warm no matter what the weather, and the window looked right onto the immaculately-maintained garden, courtesy of their friend and gardener, Pete. The girls sat in silence for a while enjoying their breakfast and the warmth of the sun they could feel touching their faces.

"I knew you were awake most of the night, Jaz" said Marie, breaking the silence. "I could feel you awake."

"I'm sorry, babe. I tried not to disturb you"

Marie reached over and clasped Jasmine's hand. "I do believe you, you know. I swear Jaz, I believe you"

Jasmine looked up into Marie's sincere eyes and she allowed herself a smile. The rest of the world may think she was a nut case but at least Marie believed her.

"Thanks. Doesn't solve anything though, does it?"

Marie avoided the question. "You'd better go and get dressed, love. We have to leave soon." Jasmine stood up, taking her empty coffee cup with her. "I do love you"

"I love you too."

Jasmine placed her cup in the sink and made her way back upstairs to attempt the task of transforming herself into a human being.

CHAPTER 2

The car felt hot and claustrophobic. Jasmine wound her window down as far as it would go and stuck her head out to feel a slight breeze blowing on her face. Marie hummed along to a Missy Elliot CD, trying to turn the volume up with one hand and steer with the other. She braked suddenly as they approached a pedestrian-crossing, narrowly avoiding an old woman wearing a heavy duffle coat despite the temperature. Jasmine pulled her head back in sharply, visualizing a decapitation or some such other horror.

"Tired of living!?" Marie hissed loudly, trying to hurry the woman across the road with dramatic hand gestures.

"She just didn't expect to meet Bristol's answer to Jenson Button on her way to the shops" replied Jasmine tersely.

Marie huffed and turned up Missy Elliot. Jasmine struggled to stay calm. After driving to work with Marie she would arrive stressed out. She knew buying the new sports car had been a mistake. Jasmine always let her drive, though. In fact she often let Marie take control of a lot of things. Marie had come back from an afternoon in town blasting a fancy horn at the front of the house. Jasmine, along with many of the other neighbours, rushed out the front door to see what all the noise was about. There, grinning like a Cheshire cat, sat Marie in brand new silver Ford Puma, bought without even consulting Jasmine.

It was only recently that such things had begun to annoy her. And now, the only time she really wanted Marie to take control, she wouldn't. That was the biggest frustration of all. As Marie sped through the busy streets of Bristol, skipping lights and singing at the top of her voice, Jasmine was thinking about the relationship. At least Marie believed Jasmine. She hadn't called her paranoid like her mother or looked at her like she had walked out of a mental institution, like the police.

As the car came to a sudden halt, Jasmine jolted back to reality, and gazed up at the imposing building in front of her. St James High School, her prison and place of work. Jasmine had attended this school firstly as a pupil and now as a teacher. She felt strangely stuck to it, like a security blanket that couldn't be put down. This school had continued to dominate her life in various ways and Jasmine sometimes longed to break free of the invisible chains holding her there. She studied the dirty stone and the old-fashioned windows, and noticed the weather worn look of the main entrance door. Forbidding shadows danced and mocked her on the door and, for a second, Jasmine wanted Marie to drive her far away so she didn't have to go in. That thought disappeared as quickly as it had come when David walked up to the car and stuck his head through the open window.

"Morning girls. Smoke room for a fag?" he asked, opening the car door and not waiting for a reply. Marie leaned over and kissed Jasmine on the cheek.

"You'd better be off" she said. "Have a good day."

Neither of the girls failed to notice the smirk on David's face. He had known of Jasmine's relationship with Marie for two years but still seemed to get a kick from seeing them together. Jasmine didn't even want to think what was going on in his head right now. What was it about men and lesbians?

They really seemed to believe that women could not enjoy a sexual relationship without a man present. Jasmine picked up her bag from the floor and got out. David was still smirking.

"You could kiss her goodbye properly you know. Don't hold back on my account." David ran his fingers through his tussled hair and smoothed down an eyebrow with his finger. He tilted his head as if waiting for a reply. Jasmine resisted the urge to punch him but instead waved to Marie as she drove out of the school. The car was soon nothing but a light in the distance. She headed towards the school entrance and David was quick to follow her, linking his arm through hers. Jasmine pulled her arm away sharply. She was not in the mood for him today...

Later, Marie sat staring at her computer but not reading the words. The office activities carried on around her, fax machines turning out sheet after sheet, the telephone ringing and high pitched squeaky voices thanking unseen people for their phone call. All Marie could see was creepy David and his immaculately-pressed suit. She hated the man ever since Jaz took her on a staff night out. The way he looked at them both, his pervy eyes speaking volumes. Most of Jasmine's other work colleagues had been pleasant enough and accepted Jasmine's new partner: sexuality irrelevant. But to David she was a source of amusement and fantasy, a little plaything that he could conjure up in his primitive little brain and tease. Jasmine didn't seem to like him very much either, but as they both worked together in the English department a working relationship had to be established.

Marie looked at the clock and her spirits sank. It was only 11.15 and nowhere near lunchtime. She had so much work to do as well but could find no motivation or enthusiasm for the tasks ahead. She had told Jasmine she had believed her this morning but the truth was Marie was not sure. This bothered her immensely. Marie prided herself on her blunt honesty, whether the recipient liked it or not. Marie swung her stool around and looked out the window. Nothing but grey and drab high rise offices looked back at her. Her office was situated on the west side of the building and was constantly shaded. Sometimes she longed for even a germ-riddled pigeon to fly by, anything to show her that life was continuing outside. She often forgot that fact while sat in this miserable and depressing dark cave.

"......as normal?" came a quiet voice, disturbing Marie's thought patterns.

"Huh?" Marie turned around to see Gina, the office junior. She always wore a shocked expression and would blush from the neck up whenever anyone spoke to her. She was wearing a grey flannel suit that did little to flatter her figure. Marie felt sorry for her. Everyone would send her on stupid errands and watch her face become like an over ripe tomato as she realised that she was being teased.

"I said, do you want your normal cake from the shop?" Gina fiddled nervously with her hair, waiting for Marie to answer. It needed a good wash.

"No thanks Gina, watching the waistline" Marie lied, smiling falsely. If it was cake time then Marie knew she could slip outside for a well-needed fag and not be missed. She had an overwhelming urge to call Jasmine.

Jasmine, resting in the staff room during lunch break, felt the vibration before she heard the ring. Taking her mobile from inside her trouser pocket she stared at the phone, unsure whether to answer it or let it ring. Answering her phone had become a big issue to her recently. She flipped up the front and placed her ear against the handset. Within seconds the hairs on her arm stood up, her senses alert and her back tingling as without needing to ask, she knew who was on the other end.

Outside in the glorious sunshine, sat on his designer jacket in a discreet and sheltered part of the school playing field, David laughed into his mobile phone.

Later, Jasmine looked at Stephen Banks as he tried to justify his lack of homework. She noticed his dirty nails and unkempt hair and she felt sorry for him. After meeting his parents on numerous occasions one could not help but feel sorry for this boy who stood no chance in life. After Stephen's two weeks of truancy Jasmine had been forced to contact them and request a meeting. They took over two months to arrive, and when they finally contacted her, she was welcomed with a tirade of abuse and blame. Both parents looked dirtier than Stephen and with even less manners and articulation. Letting out a big sigh Jasmine tried to focus on Stephen but failed miserably.

"Do it tonight, Stephen, and hand it in first thing tomorrow morning" Jasmine knew she would not see him again for the rest of the week and guilt struck her hard in the chest. She should really sort this problem out but after the phone call earlier she felt a lack of control around anything.

"Ta miss" Stephen replied, a look of relief on his face. "I do that." Stephen walked back to his desk and Jasmine looked at his too short trousers and ill fitting shoes from behind. Sometimes she wondered why she did this job.

It was 9 o'clock and Marie was shattered. She was sitting on the big white leather sofa next to Jasmine and looking forward to watching some mind numbing T.V where she could unwind and spend some quiet time with Jasmine. She hadn't got home until 7pm; Jasmine had grabbed a lift from David. That annoyed her and Marie was angry at herself for feeling like that. Why should it bother her that a colleague's of Jasmine had driven her home? Marie knew the answer.

"So was the creep pleasant on the way home?" Marie asked, instantly regretting her choice of words.

"Why, Miss Andrews, do I detect a hint of jealousy in those words?"

"No, but he is pervy, Jaz, and I don't like to think of him making you feel uncomfortable"

Jasmine took hold of Marie's hand. "I can handle him Mer; don't let him wind you up."

Marie was not satisfied but decided to drop the subject. She took her hand away and reached for her own glass of wine. "God, I need this." She took a long gulp from the glass and stole a sideways glance at Jasmine. She really is beautiful, she thought, taking in the sight of Jasmine's jet black long hair and startlingly blue eyes. Jasmine felt Marie's eyes boring into her and turned her head. Their eyes met and held together until Jasmine spoke and broke the spell.

"I had another call today. I think I did anyway…they never speak, just like always, but it felt the same. Withheld number as usual."

"Shit. Are you sure?" Marie asked, feeling anger well up inside. She didn't know if she was angry at the 'mysterious caller' or Jasmine.

"Well, it was the same as usual, no talking, just silence. I hung up as soon as I realized."

"Was it lunchtime?" Marie asked, a thought suddenly jumping into her head.

"Yes, how did you know?"

"Because I tried to call you at lunchtime and your phone was engaged. Must have been when the weirdo was calling."

"Must have been" replied Jasmine. "Mer, what if he knows where I live?"

"He doesn't babe, I'm sure of it" Marie answered, unaware that she had pulled her cardigan tighter around her torso as a form of protection. "You said yourself you might just have been paranoid because of the calls. You haven't mentioned anyone following you for a while now."

"I…oh I don't know what I think anymore. I haven't sensed anyone following me for a while I must admit. Oh Mer, these calls are freaking me out."

"It is going to be O.K, Jaz. Trust me. We'll go and change your phone again at the weekend, get you a new number."

Jasmine nodded at her doubtfully. She had changed her phone a few weeks after the calls had started and for a while they stopped, only to start up again.

"Yes, OK, that's what we will do" Jasmine placed her head on Marie's shoulder. She knew she had to stop letting the calls freak her out but it was difficult.

Marie rested her head on Jasmine's and shut her eyes. What was going on, she thought? And more importantly, what the hell could she do about it?

Gemma Middleton

Revenge is a dish best served cold

The black transparent chemise clung to her rounded breasts, tumbled down past her stomach and ended at the top of her thighs. She caught sight of her reflection in the mirror. Through the fabric she could just see the sliver of her stretch marks. It looked to her as if her nipples were straining to have a conversation with her belly button. She reached for her bathrobe, instantly warmed by it, feeling secure in its hold.

She returned downstairs to the kitchen and the ruined meal. The lettuce in the prawn cocktail had begun to go limp. The beef bourguignon lay congealed in the casserole dish. She decided to go straight for dessert. Cutting herself a substantial portion of chocolate cake and pouring another glass of red wine; third one tonight, but who's counting.

He had promised to be home early. Ten years of marriage was something to celebrate. He'd been working so hard recently; it couldn't be good for him. Most nights he wasn't home before 10 but surely this evening they could have spared him?

She bit into the cake, feeling its soft moist texture in her mouth. The combination of chocolate and wine soothed as it went down. She remembered Jenni Murray on 'Woman's Hour' saying that for some women a chocolate fix was a good as an orgasm. She couldn't recall the last time his hands had touched her body. Taking another mouthful of cake she could feel the chocolate coating her teeth, sticking to every corner of her mouth. It gave instant satisfaction, soft, sweet and sensuous. She was beginning to get into this. Just then he walked in, empty-handed and unsmiling.

"I don't love you any more. I want a divorce." She couldn't quite grasp what he was saying as the cake was still having its effect.

"Sorry, what did you say?"

"It's over. I'm leaving."

She heard him clearly this time and the words hit like a physical blow. It must be some sick joke; they had been together so long.

"You can't be serious. What about the children?" Her voice was beginning to tremble; she swallowed hard to try and keep her composure. It was their wedding anniversary, you give flowers or cards. She wasn't expecting diamonds, but to announce....

"Why?" She said.

"There is someone else. I didn't mean for it to happen. We work together and over time..." he broke off realizing that the details probably weren't needed at this moment.

"What, you bumped into her one day in the office and whoops, your penis slipped into her. I presume you have been sleeping with her because you sure as hell haven't been doing it with me?"

He turned away. She was so angry. She had ironed over 1800 shirts for him, prepared 100s of meals. Ten Christmas dinners had been cooked for his ungrateful mother, accepting criticism as if they were gems from a box. Shopped, cleaned, washed, and decorated, sympathetic ear, soothed, loved, groaned and moaned in all the appropriate places. Now she was to be disposed of with the prawn cocktail. No, she wasn't going to let it happen. She wanted him to feel pain, to do a 'Bobbit', cutting off his manhood and stamping on it. But no. Was he worth the waste of energy? The mess? Bloodstains are so difficult to get out, she thought.

She looked over at the chocolate cake, it was now beginning to sweat with the heat of the room; its dark brown coat glistened and shone. It was tantalizing; as if it was flirting with her. With a new

found strength she held his gaze, looked into his empty eyes and said:
"So you won't be wanting your chocolate cake then?"

Alison Killeen

Stars

I am looking at the stars and wondering about space. A bizarre thing to be thinking about, you may well think, and yes, given my circumstances, space should be the last thing on my mind. But it is, so please be patient with me. I can't quite decide why stars are there, really. My mother told me they were angels and for many years I believed my deceased grandparents could see me. Of course, with maturity comes harsh reality. Ok, so understanding that stars are other planets is a worthwhile thing to know but to an optimist like me, I want to believe that the human race lives on in the sky and to be able to come out to check on my loved ones after dark.

You're wondering why my head is full of this irrelevance, but I know why. I should be planning what little time I have left, but that's not my style. I'm more interested in what's up above. Or to be more precise, what's not. I guess this is where the stars come in at the moment. I would rather believe I will still see all the people I love from afar. How does a spirit become a star anyway? Do we glow silver in the dark and hide behind the clouds during the daylight? It's easier for me to think about stars. You see, for me, what happens after death is really the underlying issue in my head. Sooner or later, whether I like it or not, I am going somewhere. What is wrong with me has no cure. A star is the only future I can wish for, just now.

Gemma Middleton

Meaning of Life

It was late one Tuesday when he walked into the cafe. He was clad in a long, blue coat, which ended just inches from the ground. I noticed his hair was unkempt as he came over and ordered a mug of tea. As I handed it over he grabbed my arm and said,

'I know the meaning of life.'

Not again, I thought. Last week we had someone claiming to be Spartacus. With that he started searching his pockets, frantically spilling the contents onto the counter. He became more desperate, his eyes looked haunted. Then he suddenly stopped, looked at the heaped rubbish in front of him, felt his empty pockets and said:

'Oh bugger! I've lost it!'

Alison Killeen

The Homecoming

The studio was dark and deserted. After the briefest sense of relief that came from the return to the familiar, she became overwhelmed by a strong feeling of panic as loneliness washed away her fragile pleasure. She flicked a switch, bathing the room in the harshness of fluorescent light. Silence enveloped her like a leaden shroud and the coldness of the unheated room began to soak through her travel-weary body.

She was home.

Around her, the room echoed of her sudden departure, made evident from the clothes-strewn floor. Drawers were hanging open, spewing forth their eclectic display, whilst beside her; a t-shirt had been tossed on the floor, along with her dignity. She had risked everything, her heart and her pride, and the gamble had been lost. Humiliation weighed heavily, as she remembered how blindly she had chased the illusion of something that had never truly been hers.

Pulling herself together, she braced herself against the coldness of reality, and with the little courage that remained, managed to propel herself toward the kitchen. Her stomach growled as she opened the door of the fridge. But this glimpse of hunger vanished, as she was assaulted by the stench of decaying chow mein and mouldering egg-fried rice. Presented with these remains of a forgotten meal, she stood quailing.

Whilst forcing herself to dispose of the rotting food, she made a mental note to empty the festering bin. Practicalities had begun to assert themselves. Picking up a milk carton, she flinched at the acrid smell emanating from the stale yellowed slime within. The congealed lumps that she tipped into the sink attempted to seep through the drainage hole into the darkness below. Observing the gunk's failed escape, she resignedly turned on the taps and, as the water washed away the greasy ooze, she felt the sudden heat of tears on her face. Both surprised and angry, she brushed them violently away.

She was alone once more.

Amanda Stone

Being a Grown-up

Grown-ups are strange. Why is it that grown-ups always tell you to wash your hands? Mummy always wants my hands to be clean but my Daddy says that it is the sign of a 'hard day's graft' to have dirt on your hands. I'm not to sure what a 'hard day's graft' is really, but if it makes me like my Daddy then I want to do a 'hard day's graft.'

When I go out playing, I like my hands to get dirty to look like my Daddy's hands. I know Mummy wants my hands clean though so sometimes, just to please her, I wash them in a puddle before I go in, but she still tells me to wash them again. She even tells me to wash my hands when I've been to the bathroom. They are always clean when I have had a poo because I sometimes get poo under my nails when I wipe my bum, and then I have to get it out with toilet roll. I make sure I clean my hands really well with toilet roll, so how can they still need washing? I think grown-ups just say some things to be bossy. Mummy is always telling me to clean my teeth, as well. I want teeth like grandma. She takes them out at night and puts them in a glass. She says that when she puts them back in, they are nice and clean. I bet you have to be a grown-up before you can take your teeth out and put them in a glass.

How come you have to be a grown-up to swear? My big sister is having a baby, and when Mummy told Daddy, he said it must have been the 'bastard' next door. I asked Mummy how the 'B' word put a baby in Gloria's tummy and she shouted at my Daddy for swearing in front of me. Then she shouted at me for saying it! Mummy said to Daddy that if I said any more swear words she was holding him responsible and would cut up his tools. I don't know how Mummy could have cut up his tools.

Daddy keeps his tools in the shed and his hammer would never break. I dropped it once and it killed my toe. When Mummy stomped back to the kitchen, Daddy made me promise not to swear again. He must love his tools. I promised that I wouldn't swear again, but that didn't seem fair, because everyone still swears all the time.

Why do grown-ups tell fibs as well? Mummy says that when you tell fibs your tongue turns into a fork, but she and Daddy tell fibs. I wanted to know how the baby got into Gloria's tummy and Mummy said that a seed was planted and now it's growing. I KNOW that's not true. Everyone knows that seeds only grow in mud, so Mummy told me a fib. I kept looking at her tongue afterwards, but it doesn't look any different. I asked Daddy the same question, and he told me another fib. He said it got there because of Cider. I know that has to be a fib too, because once, Daddy gave me some of his Cider, and I never got a baby in my tummy.

I think grown-ups have the best time. They can eat what they want, stay up late and get to boss children around. I can't wait to be a grown-up. I'm going to eat sweets all day, and stay up really late, like 10 o'clock, or something. Even though grown-ups can do anything, they never smile much. My Mummy and Daddy never even laugh at Scooby-Doo, and he is well funny. I think I might practise at being a Daddy when the new baby comes. I will be eight years older than the baby, and I'm going to boss it around ALL THE TIME. I'm glad Gloria is not my Mummy though. She's horrible. I think she's a grown-up now, but I'm not sure. I might ask her, but I will have to wait until she's not 'stressed'. I don't know what 'stressed' is, but I don't ever want to be it. Gloria cries when she is 'stressed.'

I don't understand grown-ups, or Gloria. They just don't make sense.

Gemma Middleton

About our Creative Writing Course

Bath Spa University is recognised as a pioneer and leading provider in the teaching of creative writing.

The Undergraduate Creative Writing Programme includes prose fiction of all kinds; poetry; scriptwriting for theatre, screen and radio; and narrative non-fiction, such as travel writing, nature writing and life-writing.

This course aims to equip you with the skills involved in creative writing for print publication, film, television and radio; for the cultural and heritage industries and for self-expression and communication in an unlimited variety of contexts. It is also designed to equip you with interpersonal skills, including awareness of tone, register, vocabulary and audience in written and oral communication, skills of listening and comprehension and skills of imagination and empathy. It encourages you to be confident, adventurous and constructively self-critical in your creative writing, and teaches you to prepare your work for submission to literary agents, publishers, broadcasters, magazines and newspapers and other professional outlets.

Every year the Creative Writing team organises a programme of visits by writers, publishers, literary agents, producers and other guests whose work is connected with creative writing. Public events such as readings, master classes, poetry slams and public workshops are organised throughout the year. Undergraduate students frequently organise and participate in these events. This course will build confidence in yourself that can be applied to any working environment and is suitable for students of all ages.

Pressed Items

Leaving Home

What is it like to leave home – Zimbabwe, the place that grew us – and settle in a distant land? Is it simply a question of exchanging one geographical location for another, consigning the past to treasured memory and embracing change? Or does nostalgic comparison and a continued sense of displacement prevent us from seeing new surroundings through anything our own culture-coloured lens?

London. It's Christmas. A season of joy and glad tidings, and yet all the more poignant for its reminders of home. When I left Harare Airport in July 2001, I did so with resolve – determined not to look back as I shuffled through the boarding gates with luggage, children and high hopes for a better future. With that conviction firmly rooted, I arrived at Heathrow in high spirits the following morning to be met with a glorious summer sky and the efficient frenzy of first-world utopia. Two hours, and one sleepy village later, I opened the door to my new home in England.

Four years on, bright anticipation has dulled into acceptance that although there are many similarities between the two, the differences inherent in my two continents divide loyalties as cleanly as the oceans that separate them. On the one hand, I am grateful for the opportunities afforded by this new life; on the other, I long for my country with the same intensity that an October veld yearns for the first of the season's storms. And the culture shock that was, still is.

Some aspects of life on what I fondly call "l'isle de gris" (the Isle of Grey) are so similar to Africa; some quite glaringly different – and it seems natural somehow to compare everything in England with its counterpart 6,000 miles away. Not only the cold and its icy tendrils of discomfort – although I have become accustomed to central heating and the need for layers outdoors – but the rain. It cascades softly, almost apologetically, here. Falling consistently throughout the year, it lacks the formidable, great, rolling drumbeats of thunder and lightning that epitomise the purple skies of home.

And things are always wet. Everywhere you look, moisture clings tenaciously; except in summer when heat mirages float above the horizon to produce an almost tangible sense of home and driving along sunny, suburban scrub feels, magically, the same as winding Africa's contours. Except there is no dust and no acrid smell of dry-earth atrophy to tease your senses; only sea breeze humidity and the taste of roadside vendors. That said, the seasons change wondrously here, from golden, sensuous warmth to russet-coloured autumn, from dark, depressing winter to vibrant, spring-filled energy. I love that.

People, too, are different. When I first arrived, I spent most of my time smiling at everyone. More concerned with decorum than window-shopping, I missed most of the local bargains in an attempt to appear friendly, eye-contact approachable and acceptable. As the years have worn on, I realise that eating a cream doughnut – noisily – on a crowded, anonymous coachful of travellers is better than trying to foist upon an unwilling audience the social niceties implicit to African culture. I have not yet fallen to spitting in the street, or hurling abuse at those older than myself, but I do find myself walking the streets of Wiltshire with an acquired air of casual disdain. And if anyone smiles at me, I wonder why.

I miss the slow-paced lifestyle of the third world. Given a choice between the bumper-to-bumper traffic that turns a 20 mile journey into a tedious expedition, and pushing my car along a potholed street to find petrol, I might choose the latter. Faced with the dilemma of how large a suitcase I'd need to carry the worthless millions needed for a week's shopping in Zimbabwe or which of the myriad cheeses I could purchase for less than a pound locally, the former would tempt me!

Last week I met a fellow Zimbabwean; someone with whom I might have had no contact once upon a yesterday. But distance is a great leveller and displacement the unifying force that binds more effectively than politics. He was a kindred spirit – of different race, culture and language, but at once familiar. And between us lay the sad, unspoken question we all ask as Zimbabweans cut off from our birthright: Can we ever go home?

It's Christmas. The shops are filled with lights and trees and decorations that shout the season's greetings. But oh, how I long for the scent of a real fir, its improvised 40-gallon container brimming with garden cones and last year's recycled tinsel. And on Christmas Eve, I don't want to watch tradition's latest horror flick – I want to weep at the story of Jesus.

Michelle Burton

Our Story

The first thing that I noticed about Rolf was his smile and then his six-pack. He was a friend of my sister and had come around on the pretence of seeing her. She was out so Rolf spent the afternoon with me, watching me doing some art homework. That was how it all began. I was 16 and he was 17. It sounds like something out of the *Sound Of Music*. We got engaged on my 18th birthday and married just before my 20th. Rolf was in the RAF and soon after our wedding we moved into married quarters and set up home together.

 We were married for about four years before we had Josh. Rolf was completely bowled over by him. I remember him crying the first time he held his son and that look of ecstasy new dads have. He was wonderful with Josh, ready to change nappies and he would spend many a night pacing the floor with him. The only thing that marred our happy family was that at about the same time Josh came along so did what we thought were panic attacks. But there was a niggling doubt in my mind because they didn't seem quite right. Rolf described them as an intense feeling of fear. I tried to get him to go to the doctor but he wasn't keen and kept saying they were nothing to worry about.

 The attacks became a part of our everyday life. Rolf got used to them, even finding them comforting in a strange way. That was until about three years later. We had gone to visit family. Rolf and Josh drove to his gran's to help stain a fence, leaving me at my mum's, as I was heavily pregnant with Joe. It was then that he had his first tonic clonic seizure and the only person who saw it was three-year-old Josh. I don't remember much about that day. I was so shocked that it's all a bit of a blur. I started to wonder if there was a connection between the panic attacks and the fit. But we were told that one fit didn't mean he had epilepsy. Rolf still didn't want to talk about the feelings he had been having and I don't think he was trying to be deceptive. I think he just didn't see how there could be a connection. He was put under the care of a neurologist at RAF Wroughton, a service hospital while I hit a bit of a blank mainly because I wasn't allowed into the consultations. I had to stay in the waiting room with the children. This made me feel like a second-class citizen and completely shut off from what was happening. Rolf would be quite emotional at these meetings and would invariably forget to say something or more importantly forget what was said.

Some months later Rolf had another tonic clonic but this time it was at work. He was then diagnosed with epilepsy. This was when our lives seemed to spiral out of control. It felt like a matter of days but I think it was actually a couple of months, or even a year, when Rolf was called to a meeting. He was told that because of his condition he was going to be medically discharged from the RAF. His 12 years of service were over in a matter of minutes. We now had to face it; Rolf didn't have a job and had a medical condition that we knew very little about. I know he isn't the first person to lose a job but it was more to us; it was a career and a way of life. Rolf hit a real low. He just couldn't talk about the way he was feeling. I became so worried and angry. We had two small children, a mortgage to pay and on top of this it felt as if he was shutting me out. I realise now that he just couldn't put into words the way he felt but at the time I couldn't see this. All we seemed to do was row or there would be long silences. Then, luckily, one of our close friends managed to get Rolf an interview at a local car fleet management company. He got the job and that was one problem solved. Rolf was very open about his epilepsy and to date people don't seem to have a problem with it.

Our second salvation came in the form of The Burden Institute at Frenchay Hospital and Rolf's new neurologist. On our first appointment, I was invited in to the consultation, a new experience for me. Not only that, he actually asked me about my feelings. At long last I began to get a small glimpse of what Rolf was going through. We found out that his type of epilepsy is frontal lobe and what we had thought were panic attacks for all these years were, in fact, complex partial seizures.

Next we started the hunt for medication that would stabilize Rolf. He would start a new drug while we waited to see if this would be the one. Initially it would take a little while for his body to get used to the drug. He would be tired and sometimes fuzzy-headed but once he was over that stage, things would look good. I would quietly count the months, daring not to hope that this could be the one. The longest Rolf ever went without a seizure was nine months. I remember hearing our son Joe telling one of his friends that we only had to wait three more months and his dad would be able to drive again. Soon after that, the seizures began again with a vengeance and our hopes were dashed. That seems to be the pattern, he will go a few months and then the attacks will start again just as before.

Rolf has rebelled a bit against the drugs over the years. He would get frustrated that he had to take them and that they didn't do what he wanted them to. Added to this, he was never really a 100% convinced he had epilepsy. I would try not to nag him about taking his medication. That was until he had his third tonic clonic. Rolf was in the back of the car, sat between the boys, as by now we had our third child, Rosie, and she was in her car seat in the front. I found out later that Rolf had gone a couple of days with out taking his tablets and this triggered a fit. We were in the middle of nowhere when it started. Josh was about five and Joe three. Understandably, they were terrified and the location made things very complicated. I had to decide whether to go back or carry on home. I decided to go back to my parents' house, which turned out to be the best decision as the children had their cousins to take their mind off things. When Rolf realised what we had gone through he was devastated. Since then he takes his medication.

We eventually got to the stage where Rolf had tried all the drugs available, with no success. It was then that Dr Bird suggested surgery. I wasn't very keen at first but felt that we needed to try all avenues open to us. So began the many tests that Rolf needed to make sure he was suitable. One sticks in my mind, not only because he had to be in hospital for 10 days, but because something happened that made Rolf finally accept his condition. He had to have his drugs gradually reduced so that they could get a recording of him having seizures. Rolf had loads of wires attached to his head measuring his brain activity. He looked like something from a science fiction movie. Rolf was able to watch video footage of himself having fits. It was very emotional for him but at long last he had to accept that he had epilepsy. It had only taken him nine years.

Before I knew it the day of surgery was upon us. When we booked Rolf into hospital his surgeon came to see us. He wasn't sure if he would be able to carry out the operation. The seizures were coming from the right frontal lobe and some of the testing had shown that this supported his memory. It all depended on where and how deep in the lobe the seizures started. Nevertheless, they would still have to get to the brain so that they could do the test, so there were still risks.

That night I was restless, full of dreams, the sort that when you wake up you feel worse than when you went to bed. I had taken a day off work which was probably the worst thing to do. I had a long day of waiting in front of me, knowing that Rolf was going to be in surgery for about seven hours. I kept thinking about the things I should have said to him, wishing I had told him that I loved him rather than making jokes to take his mind off things. I tried to be strong for the children but they could see that I was worried. Rosie was only five and didn't really understand what was going on. I just didn't know what to say to make it better for her. All afternoon I was desperate to phone the hospital but I managed to wait till four o'clock. By this time he was back on the ward and doing fine. A weight lifted from my shoulders. Later on Rolf phoned me, he was very groggy but it was so good to hear his voice. He said they were unable to take any of the frontal lobe. This would mean further testing before surgery could be considered again. I wasn't sure if I could face another day like that.

After long discussions, we have decided that Rolf won't go for surgery. For it to be viable he would have to have more intrusive testing which in itself holds risks. Also there are no guarantees that the surgery would be successful. After all, the medication that he takes controls tonic clonic seizures. He is able to work, the only thing he can't do is drive. But the main reason for our decision was the effect it had on the children. For some time after Rosie, a normally confident and happy little girl began to get upset about little things at school and the boys were more affected than they would admit.

Rolf says that he has accepted that his epilepsy won't be controlled but I think we both still hope a cure will come along. He does get depressed and some days it's as if someone has thrown a black blanket over him. We know that it's due to his epilepsy and the drugs, but it still affects all of us. We have now been married for 20 years. Rolf's six pack is a little buried, along with my 24 inch waist, but his smile is still the same. Epilepsy has had a big impact on our lives but it is only a very small part of the person that Rolf is. I thank my lucky stars that all those years ago he took such an interest in my art homework.

Alison Killeen

PND – The Silent Illness

"I was stood at the sink washing up late one afternoon. The hot water ran over my hands. The next thing I remember, it was dark outside, and my hands were blue. I thanked God I lived near a train station because I could easily throw myself onto the tracks."

This harrowing statement came from a first-time mother suffering from PND, more commonly known as, postnatal depression. Postnatal depression affects one in 10 mothers and often goes undiagnosed and untreated. PND follows no rules. Many suffer in silence for fear of having their baby taken away or looking like a failure to family and friends. Anyone can suffer from it after the birth of a child, even if they have given birth to children previously with no symptoms.

Emma, a 33-year-old mother-of-two, recalls her harrowing experience as "the epitome of hell". A professional woman who appears full of self confidence and with an aura of determination around her, Emma did not always feel this way. She explains that she gave birth to her first son at the age of 24, and adapted to motherhood easily. "I loved it. I felt like a natural mother." Unfortunately, it was not the same experience for her after the birth of her second son, now aged three.

Emma separated from her husband when she was 26. "I didn't mind, really, I felt like a single mother anyway. He spent all his time in the pub, never with me or my son." She stayed in the marital home and ran her own successful hairdressing salon as well as bringing up her son alone. "I coped. I had good family and friends and my son was an easy child. I had a happy and fulfilling life."

Things changed for Emma, when two years later, she fell in love with Raul. Emma had known

Raul as a friend for 10 years and thought she 'knew him well.' They started dating and married a year later. Within three months she was pregnant again.

Postnatal depression is often a combination of many factors. It can be purely hormonal, brought on because of major changes after giving birth. It is thought to be more common in mothers who have a history of depression. Stressful life events during pregnancy, lack of support at home or if the baby was unplanned or not-wanted are issues that can also contribute to PND.

Throughout her pregnancy, Emma endured frequent visits to the hospital, often resulting in an overnight stay. She was suffering from severe sickness that did not stop at the normal 12 weeks. Emma records this time as "horrendous. I missed my life. And Raul was angry with me." Her relationship with Raul was "turbulent" and Emma said that he could be very aggressive towards her. "He got angrier as the pregnancy developed. He thought I should be happy to be pregnant."

Prenatal depression can sometimes happen during the pregnancy and will normally develop into something worse after the birth. This is a feeling of depression that happens during pregnancy and can also be brought on by hormonal changes in the body. Some mothers ignore these feelings for fear of looking like a bad person.

"You are expected to be overjoyed when you are pregnant," Emma says. "It's hard to tell somebody you are desperately unhappy." If prenatal depression is recognized during a woman's pregnancy, things can be done to help. Sometimes just expressing your feelings and talking about them can make a big difference. In other cases counselling may be an option, or if needed, medication. A doctor will know what anti-depressant are safe to take whilst pregnant, and it is better treated before the baby arrives.

This is not to say that all mothers with stressful pregnancies or unsupportive partners will develop postnatal depression. Some mothers will continue after a difficult pregnancy to give birth and have no symptoms whatsoever.

PND usually develops within the first month of giving birth. It is more severe than the common 'baby blues'. Baby blues is a feeling that most mothers go through after the first few days of giving birth. The mother may be tearful, irritable and feel gloomy. It normally only lasts for a few days. PND can sometimes occur after the baby blues if a mother's mood does not lift, or becomes worse. Symptoms of postnatal depression include: persistent feelings of sadness, crying for most of the day, lack of appetite and panic attacks. Emma remembers having a panic attack in bed after returning home from the delivery ward. "I was petrified." She said.

Some mothers become so distressed that in severe PND suicidal thoughts become an everyday occurrence. So many women suffer in silence for a variety of reasons. The most common is a fear of the baby being taken away. This will never happen. Postnatal depression is a recognized medical condition and is easily treated once diagnosed. Unfortunately, society has an expectation on women to feel overjoyed at giving birth. There are preconceived ideas that all women are natural mothers, but the reality is not so. Like any new skill, motherhood is also learned through experience.

Emma said she suffered in silence for a month, and by this time her postnatal depression was so severe she made an unsuccessful suicide attempt. Raul did not understand what was happening to her and became angry and aggressive. "He would push me away when I begged for a cuddle," she said. Emma first confided in her health visitor. "Luckily we got on well. I trusted her." From here, her health visitor encouraged Emma to visit the doctor who Emma calls "amazingly supportive".

Unfortunately, Emma had left it so long before getting help that her PND developed into a more severe form, postnatal psychosis. "I hallucinated and saw spiders running over my baby's face". Emma's doctor put her on anti-depressants and referred her for counselling. "It was not just because of the birth. I knew there were other issues," she remembers. Emma's family were very supportive and she and the children went to stay with her parents for a while. Gradually Emma began to feel better but the move to her parents signified the end of her marriage. "I just did not want to go back".

Emma's story is an extreme case. Postnatal psychosis only affects 1 in 500 PND sufferers but it shows what can happen if postnatal depression remains unrecognized in mothers. PND is treatable and with the right help and support can be overcome. Mothers need to be encouraged to voice their fears and seek supportive help. Treatment does not just include medication. Counselling and therapy is often needed as well. Three years on Emma's life has changed around. "I am now on minimal anti-depressant drugs and am half way through a degree course. Life is great". Emma is also in a long-term relationship and her children are thriving. She is proof that life can get better after PND. No woman need suffer in silence.

Sufferers of postnatal depression need understanding and support, but first, women need to find the courage to speak about their feelings.

For help and advice contact:

Association of Postnatal Illness helpline: 020 73860868
National Childbirth Trust: 08704448707

Gemma Middleton

An African Container

To ship, or not to ship? The question that lingers longingly when emigration is imminent. Does one de-clutter with a vengeance and leave with suitcase only, or does sentimentality reign and Grandma's old hand-me-downs suddenly become infinitely precious? What are the highs and lows of beginning an English adventure amidst the contents of a 20-foot Africa-shaped container?

To ship was my watchword. Leave Africa without my chattels and china? Not me. After all, each and every one of my belongings had great value. My children had grown up around the long, refectory table – spent hours scribbling equations into its wooden surface as they studied, celebrated birthdays around it since they were old enough to sit, and waged fierce battles of Monopoly atop its impartial length. Desks and dressers alike had been lovingly amassed over the years, their pine and oak skeletons worthy guardians for books and old bottles and myriad collectibles that simply could not be left behind. And so they were packed.

Carefully enclosed in mountainous quantities of bubble-wrap and cardboard, fitted together in military fashion to ensure that no container space was left unfilled, I added to their number. A tiny slice of every memory found its way into the boxes. Stone carvings from Borrowdale sidewalk, bottle-top baskets from Doon Estate, cotton sheets from Ruwa and even a box of Sitra mosaic floor tiles for my 'one day' own-home. It was easier to leave then. Knowing that home was on the other side, my journey across the seas was made more secure. Anticipation reigned. Until I unpacked.

What I had conveniently forgotten was that English houses are not like African houses. They are smaller. Much smaller. So much smaller, in fact, that I could probably have furnished three homes. Instead, I put to work every creative idea I could muster in an attempt to fit the contents of a farmhouse into a Wiltshire semi. Glances from inquisitive neighbours, first bemused and then positively uproarious, spurred my efforts and one haggard week later, the task was complete.

All around me hung the smell of Africa; a tangible, dust-laden clinging that pervaded everything; a smoke and woodfire essence that permeated our English walls and gave comfort. On the undersides of cupboards were cobwebs from home – silvery threads once frowned upon and swept away, now lovingly avoided by the duster. On the back of a mirror clung a red-clay hornet's nest, empty of its fiery warriors but tenacious in its efforts to stay put. And at the bottom of one of the cartons, a desiccated mouse; not quite but almost in taxidermist's prayerful supplication. Death by disappointment, perhaps – the knowledge that there would be no room at the inn? For there was no room at all. Not even for human inhabitants.

The house bulged at the seams, groaned audibly at its sea-borne cargo, and we became practised in the art of manoeuvre. In fact, we took on positively crab-like characteristics, passing each other in skilful sideways dances on the stairs, in the passageways, around the table and through the doors. Queues outside the bathroom never formed; there was no room. Television was watched in relays, and even mealtimes had more than a second sitting. Within the heart of rural Wiltshire I had established a corner of

Africa, a mini shrine to the culture of home, an Aladdin's cave of rustic wonders – but a narrow maze of habitable space more suited to furniture store than family home, and a nightmare to keep clean.

Today there are still pictures on the walls, books on the shelf, old bottles on the trunk and candlesticks on the dining table, but much of the past has gone. Relegated to the attic, or the garage, or passed on to the children who have left, the chattels I once treasured have dwindled. In their place is a new-found realisation that life is too short to spend it polishing, space too valuable to clutter with possessions, and time too precious to waste on the wanting. This year will be better. This year I will not partake of enervating ritual or surrender spring to zealous endeavour; I shall simply enjoy the glorious flowerings, discard a little more of yesterday and remind myself I should really have brought just a suitcase.

Michelle Burton

Treat the Habit or Punish the Crime?

Sixty one percent of drug users are reconvicted within two years of release from prison. And as many as 70% of all prisoners used drugs up to 12 months prior to their prison sentence and over half of all prisoners claim they used drugs while inside. This is a harsh reality facing our society and raises the issue of how to tackle such a problem?

I spoke to Jon, a reformed drug user and frequent visitor to prison, who told me that if he had been sent to a normal prison, he wouldn't be talking to me now, he would have died. Looking at Jon, a well-mannered man working in a professional environment, I find it hard to imagine him taking drugs or breaking the law. He is gentle and as I watch him working, he exudes compassion towards his clients. Jon tells me he is 38 and has been drug-free for five years, but goes on to explain that achieving all that he has would not have been possible if he had not been given the chance to "kick the dragon."

Jon told me he escaped death purely by facing yet another term in prison. He remembers the day vividly, having spent the previous two days in court awaiting sentencing. Jon was about to be sent down for a fifth time and was expecting to receive a six-year sentence, but the judge commented on the fact that prison did not seem to deter him from crime.

Jon replied: "I need help to get clean. I steal to feed an addiction." This statement led Jon into a relatively new rehabilitation programme and from there his life turned a corner.

Jon tells me that an addict has no other option but to steal and some have addictions that can cost 100s of pounds a day. Once you are addicted, the body cannot function without a hit and obtaining that drug becomes a matter of life or death. Jon still has no recollection of his last crime because he was "as high as a kite" while stealing a car.

"I did not even know I had taken the car until some police knocked on the window and dragged me out. I did not know where I was or how I ended up unconscious in the driver's seat."

Jon tells me that he would've stolen the car to sell on the stereo and any other parts he could trade for cash. "Feeding my heroin addiction was my only focus," he says, with his head down. "I know exactly how my clients feel".

I can tell he is ashamed of his past as he fiddles with his cuffs and sleeves, avoiding my direct stare. It is hard to imagine that a drug could drag someone down to such a low existence, but it does.

The government is aware of the correlation between drug addiction and crime. In fact John Penrose, the MP for Weston-Super-Mare, has admitted his town's huge drug problem has been linked with over 93% of local crime. Steve Pilkington, ex-Chief Constable for Avon and Somerset police, admitted back in 2003 that drugs were directly responsible for soaring crime figures in Bristol.

It does not make sense that drug users are put into prison where Jon claims "drugs are readily available." He tells me that as long as you have something to sell, drugs can be obtained. "I've sold my body for a bag of brown," he says, in a matter of fact tone. I feel an overwhelming sense of pride that he can talk about his experiences with such honesty. Jon now works as a counsellor, helping other addicts overcome their addiction, putting something back into society, and helping the overlooked members of the public that others choose to ignore. But Jon still thinks not enough is done to support addicts.

"Most people do not understand that you are not a bad person. Addiction is an illness."

Jon tells me his extensive rehabilitation programme turned his life around. Jon had to adhere to strict rules and knew if he relapsed he would have been taken off the programme and put back into prison. "I lived in the centre for seven months and they re-housed me after that. The staff also helped me go back to college and train as a counsellor. I work for the same rehabilitation centre now."

Unfortunately, funds and resources are very limited and these kinds of rehabilitation centres are not available to all addicts. The government need to take a different approach to criminals with addictions and the misuse of drugs in prisons needs to be acknowledged. It is pointless to lock addicts up in a place where they can still obtain drugs. Jon is proof that addicts can recover and prosper. If things continue as they do, our society is facing even higher crime rates and countless drug-related deaths that could have been easily avoided.

Gemma Middleton

Sleep Deprivation

The problems started with the arrival of my children. First, a boy to pigeon-pair my six-year-old daughter. Then, 14 months later, a bouncing set of twins. And barely 20 months after that, offspring number five. With daytimes, night-times and all the in-between times regulated with supreme efficiency to the routine tasks of my large family, sleep and the need for it were relegated to the pto section of my hastily scribbled to-do list. I simply did not have enough time to indulge in the luxury of that particular pastime. The feeding, changing and coddling cycle that turned nights to days and days to insufficient nights as I tried to snatch a few hours of sleep between chores, became a pattern that reversed my natural body clock. It made sleeping in the dark an impossibility - an unfamiliarity – even years after my children had grown up. And this has had quite devastating effects in terms of my concentration, emotional stability and well-being.

When my monthly sleep hours amounted to the equivalent of what I should have enjoyed in a week, I decided to take action. Surviving on no more than two or three hours of midday siesta when kindly neighbours and staff kept watch over the toddling legions, my sleep was nonetheless fitful. Neither blackout curtains nor the unplugging of the telephone allowed my maternal instinct complete reprieve, and I often abandoned my attempts after an hour. In fact, the situation got so bad that I seemed to continually dissolve in a kind of meltdown. Tearful, irrational and feeling completely detached from my physical self, I would collapse once every couple of weeks into an almost unconscious limbo, then wake feeling invigorated – and wait for the cycle to begin again.

So, with the zeal of Jason in search of the Golden Fleece, I set about regulating my sleeping habits.

A trip to the doctor was my first port of call; an aged practitioner who smiled benevolently and advised me to relax! Then, I took a trip to the dustier, less well-thumbed section of the local library's journals on scientific research. Brimming with facts and figures – most research into the cause and effect of sleep deprivation has centred mainly around men and some terrifying figures that show women are more susceptible to the risk of heart attack when subject to long-term sleep deficit – I thought it wise to investigate further. A snippet of BBC Africa's morning news bulletin that talked of 'definite correlation between post-natal depression and lack of sleep' above the dawn chorus of fractious, hungry babies galvanised me into somewhat frantic action. On top of all the other problems, I certainly didn't want to be dealing with depression.

Within a few weeks, my bedroom resembled an Aladdin's cave of remedies. Herbal tinctures, shiny new editions of magazines promising dreamland utopia and token prescriptions still partially complete vied for space with lavender-scented pillows, hot-water bottles and even whale music. Recommended cures all tried, tested and found wanting. Nothing worked. I slept less and worried more; tossed restlessly and reverted to pacing the warm, moonlit corridors like a nurse on night vigil. Eventually, I gave up. I learned to live with it. And somehow, I managed to grow my family and keep heart and soul together.

In recent years, I have tried once again to reverse my sleep pattern, not really because I feel the need to, but because of the horrified looks I get when people hear that I sleep for only three or four hours a night. Out from the darkest recesses of the attic have come the dusty journals and remedies; their number added to with each new scientific cure-all as soon as it hits the headlines. However, alternating between the zombie-like paralysis of sleeping pills and boredom-induced relief provided by scanning lifeless volumes of encyclopaedias, I have never quite managed to find the 'middle ground', the healthy 8-hours-a-night slogan of the white coat brigade. And the years of relentless pursuit have brought reward of another kind; not sleep itself, or the comfort of another cure, but the decision to end my quest and allow my body its own timetable. I've given up. Instead of worrying about it, I just busy myself with things that need to be done; paperwork, letter-writing, reading – even housework, although I feel a little silly vacuuming at four in the morning. Most importantly, it brings some glorious 'me' time.

I wonder if I am unique in this strange phenomenon incomprehensible to most people? No, I don't think so. There are countless others who suffer the same isolation, though perhaps for different reasons and sleep deprivation is something we all experience at some point in our lives. From high-flying professionals to exam-anxious students, nervous newly-weds to unfulfilled retirees, we each have triggers that interrupt nocturnal bliss.

For mothers, the underlying cause is more than merely having to stay awake when the rest of the world slumbers; it is also the search for quiet time – the stillness that descends when family responsibilities are complete and we can enjoy reflective time with ourselves. It's like sitting in a warm lamp lit pool of silence, with nothing but the night sounds and thoughts for company. It is the very best time of the day. This then may be the key, the long-term panacea to a problem pills and potions simply cannot address.

Michelle Burton

Rebel with a Menopause

You've reached your 40s, covered the ground from young to young-at-heart and made it to respectability; the middle years, with all the trappings and aspirations society expects. And you're content. Or are you?

Your children have left – gone to pursue their own ideals. Your mortgage is healthy, your car synonymous with peer-group success. Your furniture is solid – your paintings original. Lace and china grace your table and Sundays are for chores. Holidays are planned – predictable – and your hobbies include pottery. Everything you have ever wanted is at your fingertips. You settle comfortably into the cardigan of familiar ritual, plan out the rest of your days with precision, make a will, bequeath your jewels and wait for retirement.

But, perhaps it is not enough. Perhaps your dreams have not been fulfilled and conformity settles about you like a shroud, rather than a warm and cosy wrap? It may well be that your bank accounts and precious heirlooms do not allow you the freedom to simply be – are merely the gilt-edged nets that trap you into the school of collective direction.

Researchers conclude that many people experience powerful emotional upheaval at some point after they reach 40. It may be to do with a sense of lost opportunities, diminished options, or growing older in an ageist society. Whatever its cause, the growing recognition that we are not young anymore causes us to question the agenda we have followed for most of our lives – and suddenly we realise it's time to change and grow and be who we want to be.

Why not break the mould – throw off the shackles of mid-life mores and live a life made simple by the absence of everything accumulated? Imagine giving up your job, selling your house, donating your goods to charity and withdrawing from the Tax God. Think, too, of a rustic shelter nestling in the foothills of a coastline, or a caravan swirled in mist and solitude, or a barge nudging on an open canal. Dream of how it might be to wake in the morning and have time to smile at the sky, go for a walk that lasts all day, or gaze into nothingness because you can. Sense the joy that comes when all you possess is only what you need!

Is this a pipe-dream? Anti-social madness? Or wisdom? Mid-life is a time of transition – the single-minded focus of youth giving way to re-evaluation and a better understanding of self. It is the perfect time to embrace the truth that life is not about material ownership – it is about ownership of ourselves.

Michelle Burton

All About Me

HOW did I get here? Well, it was a dark and stormy night in 1968. Inside the house, little stirred – but something was going 'squeak, squeak, squeak, squeak' and stirring me from playground dreams, just like it did every Friday night.

I shouldn't complain; the rusty bedsprings groaning under the coupled weights of my babysitter and her boyfriend were, though I didn't know it, to propel me down this writer's path. My innocent account of broken sleep, written days later for a Grade III English class, was pinned to the school notice board for all to admire - including my mother, whose blushes passed into legend. Inspired by this appreciation (though it was many years before Mama revealed why her face went red), I gave full reign all through school to my literary leanings, putting pen to paper at every opportunity, anything to feed my love affair with the English language. Short stories, long stories, poetry - all were grist to my mill. But with a writing career seeming to beckon, fate guided me elsewhere, into marriage and commitment to an increasingly extended family.

Many years later and another dark, stormy night marked by lack of sleep: unsettled by the prospect in 2001 of leaving forever the troubled land of my birth, Zimbabwe, I sat to try to write my way back to peace of mind - charting in words my life's journey so far. The sun rose over a coffee-stained desk and 50 pages of condensed memoir. The experience had been cathartic, liberating and deeply satisfying, and my mini-tome crossed the sea with me to my new home, England. So here I am, in a sense at full-circle, a wet, starless sky again giving inspiration to my words. My night's work (okay, it took a bit longer to knock it into shape) opened the door for this 'mature (stop laughing) student' to gain a place on a creative writing degree course and contribute – fearfully - to this anthology. So now you know.

Michelle Burton

Dirty Linen

The Afterbirth

I came into this life as a supermarket deal, "Buy One, Get One Free." I was the freebie; snuggled behind my twin sister, tucked away from prying eyes and stethoscopes. As it was the sixties, 1966 to be exact, a routine scan wasn't carried out and women were actually allowed to give birth in the comfort of their own homes. To assist they had not only a midwife but also a doctor whom you didn't have to book three weeks in advance. So my presence remained a well kept secret between my sister and me, sharing our confined space. That was until the nine months were up and our peace was broken.

I can only begin to imagine the shock the doctor had. Thinking that all the pushing had finished and the job was completed, she was then faced with another baby to be delivered. My mother had less of a chance to feel stunned. Not only was she told there was another baby but that I was breach and had to be delivered as quickly as possible. After fifteen minutes of hard labour, I came in to this world feet first. Later, when I was about 13, I made up for any distress that I may have caused the doctor. My twin and I had grown like opposites. She was tall, confident and intelligent. I was short, shy and artistic. Thirteen is an age full of awkwardness and I was part of a pair that didn't match.

The weekly food shop was a grind that our mother had to endure and even though we were teenagers, our rebellion had not stretched as far as hating our mum. So my sister and I would join her in the delights of the supermarket; facing the rows of tins and bustling people. It was on one such excursion that we met the doctor who had delivered us. She was now grey but nevertheless sprightly. She took great delight in greeting my mother and sister. Saying "it's been a long time" and "how you have grown".

Then she turned her attention to me and at the top of her voice said, "Ah, this must be the afterbirth!" It felt as if the whole of the shop had come to a brain-numbing silence. Everyone had stopped what they were doing and seemed to be looking at me. Even the Jolly Green Giant had broken from his pose on his tin of sweet corn. Mr Sheen had bought his aeroplane to a crashing halt. Snap, Crackle and Pop jostled each other on their box of Rice Krispies so they could get the prime position. They were all trying to get a better look at this freak of nature. There isn't really much you can say to a greeting like that. So I just smiled and tried to melt into the background, whilst positioning myself behind my sister. After this I didn't go shopping for a while.

Many years later when I gave birth to my first son, I was a little shocked by the practice of the midwife showing you the afterbirth. This is apparently so you can see that it is complete; if any is left behind it can make you very ill. Initially I thought this was adding insult to injury, especially after seven hours of labour. But in fact I was strangely reassured, especially when it didn't resemble a baby in any way.

Alison Killeen

Childhood

I walk through the corridors with ease. The parquet floors still smell of beeswax polish and paraffin. The high brass handles shine on the panelled doors. The dining room houses my mother's sewing machine, and my nose is still pressed against its double French-doors as I watch the rain on the Msasa trees lining the driveway send the glorious blue-headed lizards scurrying for shelter. The thunder will come soon; great, rolling drumbeats of sound as the dark and heavy clouds clash in lightning fury to announce the start of the summer rains. And the air will be filled with the acrid taste of red-clay dust and raindrops mixing in mid-fall, tumbling heavily to the dry and thirsty earth. On and on and on it will go, until the cumulus burden is lifted.

  My bedroom has not moved from its place at the end of the passage, next to my parents' room and facing the back garden. I can see my swing; an old tractor tyre suspended from rope on the gnarled under-bough of the avocado tree. It is worn now – perished by the sun – but still drifts in circular motion as the breeze rises. My sandpit is next to the garage; its brick surround keeps watch over the buckets and spades of yesterday. Washing floats gently on the line, the soapy aroma of Cookie's white canvas uniform mixing with electric air to carry far beyond the garden. There he is. Propped on a makeshift stool of old bricks from the shed, he sips his tea slowly – the hot, sweet liquid he makes once a day in an empty syrup container to wash down thick chunks of buttered bread at teatime. His eyes are closed. His dark skin soaks up the November sun and he dreams of home as the minutes tick slowly back to household duties.

Flies hum lazily on the windowsill; clustered in formless droves, they flit at the glass for escape. High up on the mantel, a spider watches – waits for his prey to tire and continues to spin the silver thread of capture. Soon, the flies will fall; spin aimlessly on their backs, wings buzzing frantically in search of purchase, and he will descend. Above the house, birds circle on the updrafts of the storm, their outstretched wings mere slivers in a purple sky.

He was a draughtsman, she a nurse. He first saw her at the local swimming pool - the open-air baths run and maintained by the Bulawayo City Council – and made discreet enquiries about the telephone number of the hostel where she lived. Unsure of her name, he described her to the person who answered, then waited slightly nervously to discover the identity of the girl he could not forget. "No, I don't think it's you I want … I want to speak to," he stammered as tactfully as he could when the wrong person came on the line, adding: "She has green eyes". Then, success. And yes, she would be honoured to accept a date with him next Saturday, knowing she would not sleep a wink the rest of the week.

When he collected her, he didn't like her shoes. She changed them. Years later my mother said she should have walked away then. But she didn't and they were married in April 1960. With nothing more than an old kist, a bag full of tennis racquets and a red Morris Minor 1000, the newlyweds set off for the utopia of the Copperbelt – the mining boom towns of colonial Northern Rhodesia.

The reality was a little different and my father spent weeks driving from one Luanshya mine to another to find work – always with the same answer: copper bonuses were high, so no one was leaving employment. His reward came unexpectedly one day at Mufilira Mine. Not on merit, for he had never worked underground before, but because he bumped into a man in the car park who noticed his socks and asked him if he was a rugby player. No, he played tennis. But incidentally, his father-in-law had worked on this very mine some years ago.

"Like 'Open Sesame'," he observed. "This fellow was the site manager and he offered me a job there and then, as a 'learner' miner." It was 1960.

The young couple bought odd bits of furniture from a certain Jimmy James and settled into their first home – a top floor flat on the Ndola Road. Later, they moved to the ground floor and, eventually, into a three-bedroomed house in the upper class 'township' area reserved for white, skilled tradesmen, shift bosses and managers. The rains came in November. I was born. And the neighbouring Congo gained its independence.

The first day of its new status was taken up with celebrations, parades and speeches; great throngs of people lining the streets to cheer and whoop and shout the ecstasy of "Freedom! ... Egalitaire!" The second day was taken up with the systematic slaughter of whites – which no one had expected.

Mufilira, until then a peaceful city, turned overnight into a bloody refuge for the mostly French-speaking Belgians lucky enough to save themselves. Bullet-holed cars filled with crying children, shocked and traumatised parents – still wearing the night clothes of flight – jerked bumper-to-bumper along the main road. A child wailed inconsolably like an animal in anguish, her father had been set alight. These former settlers had lost everything. Numerous open-air meetings at the mine club urged miners to return to the Congo, promised a cessation of hostilities and a return to calm. But most of the families never returned. Some, desperate for the few pounds needed to begin a new life, resorted to selling their vehicles. A father of three walked into one of the cafes on the High Street, asked if anyone would buy his car so that he could feed his family, and settled gratefully for the offer made by a patron with ten pounds to spare. Years later, my father was chosen to represent Mufilira in a tennis tournament against some of the whites still living in the Congo. Post-Independence, life was not much better. People were still frightened – still subjected to night raids by rebels demanding 'firewood' in the form of tables and chairs, and still fearful enough of retribution that they huddled together in clans for safety.

The mine itself was a deep, dark and dangerous place. From the bowels of the earth, rock was hoisted thousands of feet by conveyer belt to the crushers – huge roller mills that ground and separated it, spewing water to the slime dams and ore to the smelter. Great metal cages carried the miners down into the fetid underground of cables, explosive and yellow-gas blasting. Comprising four compartments, one on top of the other, the cage mirrored hierarchical status. Black workers travelled in the top three sections; white artisans, foremen and managers in the lowest. And getting a place early was important, before the weight of the top three sections lowered the doorway of the last to an impossibly narrow entrance. As important was the mood of the crane driver who released the brake and dropped the miners into dungeon oblivion. If he had a hangover, or was tired or hungry or both, he might let the cage go – allowing it to drop until the small white balls, called lilies, spun furiously and the brake registered in mid-fall. The sensation of being tossed like a yo-yo had men screaming, wetting themselves in mid-stage trip and lying prone in prayer on the cage floor.

After Independence, black workers were promoted to better jobs and upgraded to travel in the bottom of the four compartments with their white – and wary – contemporaries. And in the darkness, prejudice had its way. As the lights went out and the cage started moving, whites lashed out with sideways punches at blacks standing nearby, throwing fistfuls of transferred rage into the nearest representation of their demise. Blacks in the cage above urinated with precision through the ventilation holes in the metal grill onto their hapless, former tormentors. It was an accepted collaboration and somehow did not detract from the camaraderie between workers of all races and culture.

Lopi Lilamano idolised my father. Not only because he treated him as an equal and let him go home early on quieter days, but because he helped to establish Lopi as a force to be reckoned with in 'the games.' The games consisted of arm-wrestling matches set up between Lopi and anyone foolish enough to think he was the pushover his scrawny stature suggested. Beating them without effort caused Lopi to leap with glee and call animatedly for his next combatant. On one occasion, he and my father were working close to the 1900 level when an engineer walked in, recoiled in horror at seeing them and yelled: "Run, you buggers … run … we're about to blast!"

With seconds to spare, they managed to reach the cage as the dynamite detonated. Many years later, water from the slime dams reached the pump chamber, burst through the hanging wall, tossed trucks aside like match boxes and flooded the entire 1900 level. A number of lives were lost that day. And on other days too, when tragic accidents occurred – when the portable hoist holding a huge oil circuit breaker collapsed and broke the neck of Lennie Joubert standing beneath it.

1964 heralded the Independence of Zambia. But the crude bloodletting of the Congo did not repeat itself - rather, a newfound pride and nonchalance towards its former regime evidenced itself in the locals. One particular incident that caused a mixture of hilarity and consternation was the confidence with which a young black woman - unable to stop her newborn infant crying - simply took out her breast, wet it with saliva, dipped it into the sugar bowl at the Cakelands Coffee House and slid it into the mouth of her baby.

Within the confines of the mine, laughter was the panacea to danger. Not only did it bond together men of different stations, but alleviated the daily discomfort of gas fumes, working conditions sometimes no more that five feet square for hours on end, and the dank claustrophobia of permanent darkness. Every Saturday morning, whoever was on shift congregated in the 1650 level workshop for tea, barbecued meat, sandwiches and games. The 'megger' was a great favourite. Coins were collected from everyone present and put into a bucket of water. Then, an electrical megger lead was put into the water – the other end tied in a loop just big enough to slip over a man's finger. The object of the game was to hook your finger through the loop, dip your hand into the bucket and try to lift as many coins as you could while someone turned the megger handle that sent sharp volts of electricity racing through your body. Another pastime was to direct the 11 000 volt cable blow lamps at the rear-end of a co-worker for a second or two, turn away quickly, and then wait for the heat to penetrate his clothing and scorch his backside. The blue air that emanated as a result was half lamp-glow, half hysterical expletive. And just bright enough to make out the culprit – my father, usually.

Life was good. When they weren't at work, men socialised with their families at the Mufilira Club. Mine employees during the week, tennis champions at the weekend, they gathered ceremoniously for pecking-order placement matches throughout all but the coldest season. And even then, really. White outfits gleaming in the midday sun, play continued well into sunset and beyond - a biased analysis of events amidst rounds of ice-cold lager was the culmination to these long and glorious days. Koos Cronje – teacher, bachelor, and close friend of the family – whose incomprehensible Dutch name paid tribute to his equally incomprehensible features (an extremely unfortunate setting of his eyes that made them both penetrating and close enough to his nose to almost be part of it), was the butt of all 'ugly' jokes at the time.

It caused Koos no pain. Quite the contrary. He proclaimed often and loudly in the club bar that he had once been given a sixpence as 'a reward' for being the ugliest person the donor had ever seen. With the money, announced Koos, went the proviso that he should pass it on only if ever he came across anyone uglier than himself. I think he still has the sixpence.

But though Koos may not have been blessed with the appearance of an Adonis, compensation had been made in other ways. For one thing, he could out-knit any of the women in Mufilira. More significantly, some will say, Koos could hold his head higher than any man in the shower after a sweaty game of tennis – and don't think the scoreline on court had anything to do with it. My mother tells the story of how my father, in an unthinking moment in the pub, was foolish enough to bet Koos ten bob he was not only inferior on the tennis court but in the trouser department too. The winner was magnanimous enough to overlook the sporting jibe and stand my father a consolation beer.

In addition to Koos, my parents had a number of close friends. Dave Kennedy's claim to fame was that his wife had been at school with Vanessa Redgrave. Wallace Hulley became, in later years, one of South Africa's top three artists. Charlie Higgs was a rotund but gregarious personality whose diminutive height never seemed to detract from his speed and grace on the court. And The Richardsons.

Older than my parents, Zephne Richardson became mentor and overseer of my mother's efforts at domesticity. More than that, she was a good friend. Babysitting became a reciprocal arrangement, either her children at our house, or both sets of under-fives in the back of her station wagon while she shopped in the middle of the busiest part of post-colonial Zambia. These excursions would have been bearable had it not been for the torrent of abuse her elder son insisted on directing at almost every black passer-by when she was away. My strategy was to curl up as tightly as I could on the floor behind the front side, hide from the possibility of sidewalk retribution and pray desperately until discipline marched down the street in the form of Mrs Richardson. Then, breathing a sigh of relief so deep it lasted most of the return journey, I would vow quietly never to let my mother send me to town with them again.

I don't remember the separation. Though I suppose I should. I don't remember tears or pain when my mother finally packed our bags and took us away. I remember, instead, sitting in an armchair in the middle of the garden while all around me packers and movers piled furniture into the back of a lorry. I remember thinking the house looked smaller now.

And I remember watching my mother's legs struggle for purchase on the lower bunk of the train compartment as she manoeuvred our bags onto the luggage rack. I remember sitting curled up in the corner on the opposite bunk – one arm around my brother Jem, the other clutching my doll. It was 1966.

Michelle Burton

A Stranger's Gift

I never knew what to buy my father for Christmas or birthdays. He had however been fortunate enough to get his most longed-for gift an amazing total of six times. Every time he ended up rejecting it.

My father's name was Alan Stone and in 1966 he was a dashing young technician in the Royal Air Force. He had not long been married to my mother, Mary, and they were expecting their first child in the forthcoming January. He was based at RAF Luqa on the sunny Mediterranean island of Malta. 1967 saw him pensioned out of the air force, sent back to a chilly UK and wired up to a dialysis machine.

These were the days when the transplantation of kidneys was a far cry from the almost routine operations they have become today. Tissue typing was still in its infancy. Dad's high number of transplants was probably due simply to his having had one of the less common blood groups, AB+. There is a strong possibility that with the medical advances that have been made since, in today's world my father might not have received most or perhaps any of his donated kidneys.

The most successful transplant that my father underwent took place in 1968 and the kidney lasted eighteen months. During this time, my father had a brief period of 'normal' life. He started light work and rediscovered his libido. Staff members of Addenbrooke's Hospital, Cambridge reassured my mother that she need not go on the pill, as even if he felt like 'doing it', he would certainly be 'firing blanks'. This is how I came into being.

Family legend has it that I am named Amanda after the stranger from whom my father received his wondrous gift. My own belief is that dad being dad, he was certainly sneaky enough to use this excuse as a ploy to trump my mother's nominations of Deborah and Samantha. Though naturally, I like my parents' story better, I grew up feeling slightly special, as if I had gate-crashed some fantastic party called life.

My elder sister and I have grown up very 'kidney conscious'. Dad encouraged us to consume loads of fluids, while he sat taking tiny sips from his rationed drinking allowance. It is surely no coincidence that when a friend did me a huge favour and I said I owed her "big-time" that I jokingly asked if she needed a kidney. Likewise my sister, when hearing about the hard time I was having during my previous relationship, offered to "sell a kidney and hire an assassin" to bump off my offending partner. I guess we grew up being very aware of how vital our renal system is, automatically associating it with financial worth. Priceless.

When I look at my four children and marvel at how all five of us would not be here except for the generosity and bravery of a single, grieving family, I thank these unseen strangers with all my heart (and kidneys). My only wish is that they knew just how life changing their gift has been.

My father died when I was twenty-one and my son Jacob, was eighteen months old. I miss him dearly. Cancer got him in the end. He never got to see my three daughters, Kelsey, Maia and Culley, but Kelsey has his smile and Maia has his eyes. And he had a little girl's kidney that gave so many the chance of life.

I am registered as an organ donor. It has become a part of the family ethos and I know that it really could enable me to give 'the gift of life.' I see it as kind of like the Kevin Spacey movie, "Pay it Forward." That's what someone did for my family and I would be proud to carry on the chain.

Now when I go shopping, I am constantly finding the ideal gift for my father and kick myself for the naff boxer shorts and knickknacks that I lovingly presented to him. But as writing this has reminded me, he had already had some very special gifts, and I would like to think that my name can be added to the list.

Amanda Stone

My Father

The emotions of growing up seem closely interwoven with my memories of my mother. She is so closely linked with the joy of discovering things about life and the agonies of adolescence. Whereas the memory of my father seems to fade into the background. He just seemed ordinary. Don't get me wrong, he isn't a bad father. It was just the way it was then. I grew up in the seventies and fathers tended still to be the main breadwinner. The new-age man hadn't been thought of yet. Also, with a family of five daughters, I think he really felt a bit out of his depth. If I were to describe him as a character from literature, it would be Mr Bennett in Jane Austin's *Pride and Prejudice*. At the first high-pitched wail, he would retreat to his study, emerging only when tissues had been dispensed and broken hearts mended.

It is only now with mature eyes that I look back and realise my father was far from commonplace. At the age of 13 he ran away to sea but had to wait until he was 16 to join the Royal Navy. He worked his way up through the ranks and became an officer. Whilst his career was in full flight he had a calling from God. So he left the Navy and went to theological college. This was made all the more dramatic by the fact that he was in his 40s with five daughters still at home. I accepted all this unquestioningly. I didn't see my parents' courage. It was such a big change; a vicar's salary would never match that of an officer in the Royal Navy. Admittedly the job did come with a house. The houses were very beautiful but they were usually damp and draughty.

Something else I never questioned was that my father had a calling from God. I just assumed he had some sort of direct line to heaven. I imagined him on the phone with God discussing his career change. This all seemed very probable to me.

My father's service background meant that he was a down-to-earth vicar. It took a great deal to shock him and he never lost faith in people. Our home became a regular haunt for local tramps. They would sit on a wooden chair in the hall and be given a warm drink and a sandwich. My father would listen to their sob stories and occasionally part with a small amount of money. He would believe their insistence that they would pay him back. Of course they never did.

His service training also affected his doctrine on preaching. His theory was 'stand up, speak up and shut up'. This meant that his sermons were usually straight to the point and short. This was something we were all grateful for, especially in the winter months. No matter how much heat was thrown at the church, the old stone walls would suck all warmth from the building. My father would carry out services with very red hands. The tips of his fingers would have a blue tinge to them. Unlike the rest of us he wasn't able to wear gloves.

As time passed my father began to look like an archetypal vicar. He lost most of his hair apart from a small amount around the edge of his head. I think that is why he started to wear hats. One which sticks in my mind is the Russian hat. Some charity shop find of our mother's. It looked like a rectangular black box that sat on his head, giving him the look of a confused revolutionary, which I'm sure wasn't the effect he was after. The Russian hat was marginally better than its predecessor, a deer stalker. It didn't have earflaps, thankfully, but the country gentleman look seemed somewhat out of place in a town location. In the winter months his ensemble would be finished off with a full-length, heavy woollen cape. At the neck it had a clasp and chain to hold it together. I always thought these were lion heads. Some years later I was quite disappointed when, on close examination, I could see they were just round bits of black metal. He would wear his cape over his cassock, usually when he had to go to an evening service. So, with his Russian hat in place, he would be in black from head to toe.

I remember one winter evening when my father was returning from evensong, there was a group of youths hanging around outside a local off-licence. Their larking about was interrupted by the vision of a figure all in black striding up the street. As my father walked the cape would billow about behind him, giving the look of wings. The vision he created was far from godly. He looked more like something in allegiance with the dark side, or something from a horror film. As he approached the now terrified group, my father slowed his step. He looked at their gaping, shocked faces and said, "God Bless you". With that, he carried on walking home.

Alison Killeen

My Childhood Memory

Parents' Evening. Those two words alone managed to install a feeling of dread in me, quite unlike anything else during the 1980s. I learned from a very young age that parents, especially my mother, did not like to hear of their children's shortcomings. Unfortunately for me, shortcomings were about the only thing my parents heard at parents' evenings. Repeated statements such as "spends too much time listening to peers than me" would repeat from my mother's mouth as she described in humiliating detail how I could improve upon my education. You try and explain to an adult that at 11-year-old hearing about who-snogged-who is far more interesting than hearing about why earthquakes happen. "Could do better" was another favourite phrase. Of course I could have, I just didn't want to. I would rather be writing a fantasy story than describing the geological attributes of Africa. I put hard work into the things that count: my interests.

One particular parents' evening will stay with me forever. It was the first time I saw understanding in my mother's eyes, a tiny glimmer that she had some recollection of her own youth and that she did not land here from Mars. I had been sent around to Mrs Simmons's while my mother (Dad always escaped the torture) put on her best frock and made her way to school. I was 11-years-old and had no doubts what my mother would hear that evening. My teacher at the time was Mr Hyde, certainly a Jekyll and Hyde character. He was on exchange from America, sent over from an inner-city school to experience cultural differences. I think he experienced 'Gemma' differences. He hated me and the feeling was mutual. He took my wit as sarcasm, my imagination as lying, and my friendliness as a deliberate attempt to lure my friends' attention from his interesting classes. Trust me, his classes enthralled his pupils as much as spending a Saturday afternoon painting a fence. Boring with a capital B. His American drawl grated on me like nails down a blackboard and I would bite my tongue as an alternative to telling him to "Shut the fuck up."

He frequently sent me out of the classroom, his idea of a humiliating punishment. My idea of heaven. Even my friends would look enviously out the door as I nonchalantly leant against the wall, imagining horrific ways that Mr Hyde would find death. Always horrific, always slow and always in my presence. I kept a writing journal at that age and he was always in it, but disguised in character using the vivid imagination I possessed.

Well, by now I expect you have a good idea of what he would be telling my Mother. I waited at my neighbour's house, every minute feeling like an hour. Previous experience had taught me that watching a clock only makes it tick slower, but my imagination was imagining my punishment after my mother heard about my antics. I would be a modern day Oliver Twist, cast out into the world with a paper bag for bringing shame upon my family, no longer deserving the protection of a place to call home. Looking back, I think I was an overly dramatic child.

Eventually my mother returned. I heard Mrs Simmons answer the door. My mother's knock gave nothing away. I was sitting on the edge of the sofa, practising my most innocent smile for when my mother walked in. I can remember my hands, wet and fiddling with the corner of my dress, my stomach knotted in anticipation.

"Gemma," my mother said from the doorway.

I prayed the innocent look was still there, that it had not slipped to become a look of the resigned.

"Gemma," she repeated. "Your teacher is an asshole."

Nothing more needed to be said. I left Mrs Simmons, holding my mother's hand and thankful for the miracle that, at the time, I could not explain.

Gemma Middleton

Chicken Noodle Soup

As a child my recovery from any illness was closely linked to the consumption of Chicken Noodle Soup. This wasn't a lovingly home-made soup. Not even anything as grand as a tin, but the packet variety, the cheaper the better. Its nutritional value was disputable but the high salt content and additives would help to revitalize my appetite.

While I was ill, my mother would turn the settee into a makeshift bed. A pillow and a duvet would be bought down from upstairs. The covers were tightly tucked around and the pillow placed on top of cushions, forcing me into an upright position. From here I would be able to watch the one and only television; I also would be close to my mother as she carried out the daily chores. The closeness to her and the cocooning effect of the warm soft cover gave me a feeling of security.

When I at last felt able to face something to eat, the soup would be emptied from its paper packet and reconstituted with a pint of water. As it slowly simmered in the pan it filled the house with a salty smell. It was brought in and placed on a small rickety table in front of me. I would begin by placing my face over the bowl; gently inhaling the steam, hoping it would have some healing properties. Then I would tentatively begin by sipping the soup, testing to see if it was going to hurt my throbbing head or catch on my throat as it went down. Regardless of how long I left the soup or how much I blew on the liquid, the first mouthful would burn the roof of my mouth.

I developed the fine art of separating the liquid from the noodles. The spoon had to be tilted and a small amount of pressure placed on the noodles, preventing them from getting on to the spoon. I would continue with this until all that was left were the noodles, carpeting the bottom of the bowl with their creamy strands. Then I would begin to eat them. A couple at a time to begin with, gently squeezing them through my teeth so that they became a pulpy mass. Then I would suck up larger amounts of them and leftover soup would flick me in the face. Eventually only one or two remained. I chased them around with my spoon and once they had been caught, there was the satisfying clank of the spoon on the bowl.

Eating complete, I lay back down in my makeshift bed. The feeling of being full made me sleepy. I knew that I would soon be well enough to return to school. Or maybe I could make my recovery last a little longer?

Alison Killeen

The Bothy

There are always places which are out-of-bounds. How can adults forget how tantalising this is to a child? Once told that a place is forbidden, it becomes at once an object of wonder to ever-curious youngsters. Like the sweets that my mother put on the top shelf in the kitchen which, naturally, I climbed up for and consumed, so I knew instantly I had to investigate The Bothy.

My school was beautiful but the trees and squirrels were taken for granted along with French and algebra. The Bothy was set within the school grounds, but just out of reach, in an area where we were never permitted. From a distance, I could see the hedge that surrounded it, concealing it from my inquisitive young eyes.

Presdales was an ex-grammar, all-girl school in Hertfordshire, surrounded by woods and still quaking from its loss of eminence. Upon starting at the school, aged 11, we were quickly told about this mysterious place that was off-limits to pupils. The folly of maturity amuses me to this day. My obsession had begun and I planned my exploration for the earliest opportunity. In truth, it continues to astound me that the Bothy was not crawling with teenage girls. Where on Earth was their sense of adventure?

Grasping the chance one day to escape the view of my ever vigilant teachers, I stole across the lawn and ducked behind the green curtain that encircled my forbidden goal. The hedges around me acted as instant sound-proofing, shutting out the hum of distant hormones. Within this outer shroud, there was a fantastic sunken garden, set within pillars and with stone steps leading down to the centre of the garden. At its heart there stood a magnificent tree from Japan, though sadly the name of its species has become lost to me with the passing of time. Beyond this was a pond, dark, stagnant and forgotten. An enchanted doorway to another world, perhaps? My daydreams flourished.

The Bothy swiftly became my favourite place as well as a secret refuge from a world often plagued with unhappiness. I would flee there whenever I could, and lose myself within this haven of peace amongst chaos. My youthful imagination was free to run wild within the tangled bushes where I learned to hide from the occasional teacher on patrol. Here was my *Secret Garden*, a land of fairies and princesses, wizards and magic: a fantasy world where I hid from the ogre of reality and the evils of pubescent females.

I spent four years at this school, many hours of which I passed happily amongst the foliage of this special place. Shortly before moving away from the area, I went to The Bothy to say my goodbyes. I hadn't been there for some time and to the superficially-mature eyes of a fifteen-year-old the place appeared diminished in size and some of its wonder was now lost to me. It had become just a garden. Yet it still filled me with a sense of tranquillity that I wish I knew how to recapture today. It was a sad farewell, but I know now that the memory of this unexpected sanctuary is best left in that part of my imagination, still seen through the eyes of a child and unsullied by the cynicism of adulthood.

Amanda Stone

Living the Life

It may only be April, but the sun is warm and bright, causing a squint in my eyes and the need for sunglasses. The quietness in the car puzzles me at first, leading me to feel that something is missing. Normally, chaos reigns in the back seat, shouts of needing the toilet and declarations of sickness, usually before I leave the car park. But now I remember the family is safely in Valencia City, enjoying tourist delights in the mild spring sunshine. I am not in cold Blighty, but in the Valenciana region of Spain and on my way to visit two friends, Gareth and David, who live in the mountainous terrain of Sierra Calderona.

My hire car, a sardine tin also referred to as a Fiat Uno, has a tough job ahead. Apparently, the only 'roads' leading to Gareth and David's home are narrow mud tracks, devoid of tarmac, markings or signposts. Their dwelling is a modernized Finca situated ten minutes from the nearest village of Riba-Roharja. The term 'village' applies loosely as Riba-Roharja consists of one shop selling meat, vegetables and bread. This shop is, in fact, a garage belonging to one aspiring local who has converted it into the only supply shop for three miles around. He leaves his garage door open all day while the locals pop in to acquire their essentials. The shopkeeper is normally in his house, drinking San Miguel and entertaining friends in his kitchen, which has a door through to the back of the garage. I make my way easily to Riba-Roharja, but from here I have no clue as to where I am going.

David had given me directions which include: "bearing left at a set of carob trees" and "not taking the track that dropped off the edge of a mountain, but the other one." David has a bizarre sense of humour and I wonder if he is winding me up, knowing that I am on my own. In between my anxiety I cannot help but admire the surrounding scenery. Tall trees, bushy and unkempt plants I cannot identify and a vastness that stretches as far as my eyes can focus. As I drive upwards into the mountains, the tin fails to deliver air conditioning, forcing me to open the window and inhale the scent of pine trees and oranges. This area is green in comparison to Valencia and the surrounding villages. I imagine it must be the higher altitude, bringing more extreme weather than the coastal area receives.

While my brain is digesting the views the track ahead just stops. After slamming on the breaks, reversing the tin and proceeding down the correct mud path, I wish more than anything that I was in Valencia with my family instead of here on the road to hell. I spend time cursing my tutor, Joe, and my life-writing project, wishing I had opted for a degree in sewing because it feels like a safer alternative to what I am doing at the moment. Eventually, after a few wrong turns at carob trees, (that, by the way, are everywhere) a couple more manoeuvres out of wrong tracks and a solemn vow to never to visit again, I eventually reach the tiny urbanization of Los Vinos Manos.

Pulling into the tarmac drive, I take a few minutes to admire what is in front of me. A Finca is a small farm with over an acre of land but not necessarily used to house crops and animals. There are around 15 dwellings scattered within half a mile or so and Gareth and David's place overshadows the other buildings, standing like a proud palace amongst homes that look more like shacks. On the top of their roof sits a satellite dish and standing up behind are two electricity pylons that, in my opinion, obscure the views of the surrounding mountains. The Finca is painted white, the sun casting shadows where the bougainvillea drapes itself seductively around the walls.

I eventually get out of my faithful tin (it did get me here after all) and start to walk to the front of the house, my feet stepping on pretty patio tiles engraved with intricate leaf patterns around the edges. Halfway to the door, I notice David lying on a hammock and Gareth sitting on a bench. David is dressed quite conservatively in knee length shorts and smart t-shirt. He always reminds me of a professional business man, regardless of the situation we are meeting in. Gareth on the other hand is wearing cut offs that obviously used to be a pair of jeans and a t-shirt with the words: "Donkeys have feelings too." It is written in Spanish and the t-shirt shouts Gareth's personality. His hair resembles a character from *The Rug Rats*, standing up on end and in desperate need of a comb. They both have amused grins on their faces and David looks at his watch. He comments on my lateness, asking me if I got lost. I lie and say the traffic was bad in Valencia. A girl has her pride.

After a glass of sangria and breathing in the clear air, tinged with the scent of the surrounding palm trees, I ask Gareth to show me around. I have known both of these men for a couple of years, ever since they persuaded me to buy my own villa while working as estate agents in a town called Chiva. My villa sits on the outskirts of Chiva, around 15 miles from here, heading south towards civilization. We often meet for drinks whenever I am in Spain, but this is first time I get to see what their home is like. I know they bought it 10 years ago when it was like the rest of the surrounding homes, run down, shabby and with no running water or electricity. I can only begin to imagine the immense amount of time, effort and money which must have gone in to produce this amazing place.

My friends have been a couple for 15 years, moving from Oxford to Spain in a seemingly effortless way, falling in love with Los Vinos and spending four years creating perfect home. Gareth gets up and starts walking. I presume I am meant to follow and he leads me around the back to show off his pool that looks so inviting in this heat. The sun has brought the pool alive, giving the water a topaz sparkle that one expects to see only in the ocean. I wish I had brought my swimming cozzie.

I am struck by the tidiness of the surrounding land, having presumed that two men would not pay attention to such detail. This is not the case with Gareth and David. The pride they have is obvious, showing in every last detail and even the tiles around the pool are devoid of dirt and grime. They have placed big terracotta plant pots and I imagine what it must be like to live somewhere you love with a passion. In all honesty, the idea of waking up here, greeted by mountains and clean air strikes me as the closest someone can get to paradise.

During my tour of the outside, I notice Gareth studying me intently and, not one to hold back, I ask why he is looking at me. He replies that he gets a great deal of pleasure from visitors seeing his house for the first time, noticing the beauty that he sees every day and sometimes takes for granted. After this statement we both become lost in our own thoughts for a few minutes, mine consisting of awe, pleasure and a hint of jealousy at the life Gareth and David live. Gareth interrupts my thoughts and tells me that during the winter the mountains are snow-capped, making the scenery even more picturesque. He tells me that he is planning to spend some time walking higher up into the Sierra Calderona because the peaks are full of protected birds and flowers that are at risk in the rest of Europe.

Gareth eventually takes me inside and kindly allows me free rein to look in my own time, take photos and scribble rough notes on my pad. I fight my nosy urge to open drawers or rifle through their wardrobes. Again, the tidiness strikes me; everything neatly put away, spotlessly clean and with a very calming feel. A huge open fireplace sits in the lounge making it the main focus of the room, despite the flat screen television and all the other modern appliances I notice scattered around. This room still looks traditional, even though I cannot imagine anyone else in the nearby vicinity possessing satellite television or an internet connection. The lounge is painted yellow, which suits the atmosphere. It does not look garish or 'over the top' but encourages one to feel at home, with a sense of belonging. I notice David's guitar on the sofa and modern English paintings on the wall. Somehow these guys have managed to combine modern and traditional in a way that does not feel false or pretentious. I have decided they would make great interior designers.

The Finca has a pleasing smell that I can only describe as homely. I can distinguish the aroma of cooking, the strong scent of the foliage outside and the faint hint of cleaning products. The building is made up of a lounge, two bathrooms, a dining area, a huge kitchen that is quite unusual here in Spain and five perfectly sized bedrooms. The fact that a large kitchen is unusual in Spain is due to the weather. In the Valenciana region the climate remains relatively mild for eight months of the year and all the cooking is done on an outside paellero, a stone built area that resembles a barbeque. The traditional dish of paella is then prepared on this, rice and meat thrown into a huge pan and left to simmer until cooked. I also notice all the bedrooms are furnished in pine and the four guest rooms are identical, even down to the clean, crisp white quilt covers. I wonder if they have a maid, but I cannot visualize Gareth and David allowing anyone else to put an imprint on their haven. Knowing both men as I do, this place perfectly expresses both personalities, with Gareth's warmth and sense of fun and David's calm laid back attitude combined perfectly.

My next quest was to use my journalistic tactics to extract some information from them regarding the attitudes of the neighbours, not just because of their sexuality, but also because of the modern way of life they have brought to Los Vinos Manos. By the time we return to the seating at the front, David has produced some hand-picked oranges and nuts that he took from the land next door. He tells me the owner of the land, Juanes, allows them to take as much fruit as they want, but it comes with a condition. Whenever Gareth and David venture to civilization, which is quite often as they possess a Landrover and a good social life, they have to bring back supplies for him.

The two men booked a cheap flight to Valencia in the summer of 1996, fell in love with the place and moved the following year, giving gave up careers and a trendy, expensive flat for what they have now. At this point David interrupts and says they first moved to Chiva and rented a flat until they found the ideal property. He tells me the Finca was very dilapidated and needed a lot of work, but it was the scenery that grabbed them. They threw off any doubts or fears they may have had about the venture, but it took four years before they finally moved in which, according to Gareth, was because David wanted things completely finished and to a standard that he could happily live in. I think the words 'anally retentive' went in somewhere as well.

Gareth tells me about the intrigue they raised amongst the neighbours. From the time they received the keys both men became entertainment figures amongst the locals due to the fact that they employed the English builders who had renovated their flat in Oxford. They paid for the builders to fly over and stay for six months at a time, but none of the team spoke any Spanish, so getting materials, equipment and any other necessities became the responsibility of David and Gareth. This memory causes both men to start laughing and Gareth tells me that eventually they had to employ Spanish builders to help because the language barrier became an issue. On one occasion they needed to hire a digger but ended up with a delivery of 100 bags of cement mix. He remembers that the neighbours stood around laughing as the builders shouted at the delivery men in English, neither party understanding the other. I imagine a stereotypical English builder in Spain, top removed and a builder's bum hanging from ill-fitting shorts.

David tells me that no one initiated a conversation with them until they had been working on the Finca for over six months. He says that both he and Gareth would try to communicate with the other neighbours in pigeon Spanish, but they would plead a complete lack of understanding until one day, Juanes, the man from next door, came up to David and asked him in perfect English if he could have a look inside and see how the work was going. David, who at this point is peeling an orange and making my mouth water, chuckles and tells me he didn't know whether to laugh at him or clock him one. He obviously made the right choice, because from this point all the other neighbours started making small talk with them and eventually friendships developed.

I start to stretch my legs and Gareth walks back inside to return with a plate of fresh bread, hams and olives. The bread has been freshly baked and the smell is mouth watering. I am grateful for the delicious-smelling food as the mangy-looking donkey in a field opposite was beginning to look appetising to me. David tells me the olives come from Juanes' own crop and the ham was a Christmas present given to them as a whole pig. The men must have looked at my face and read disgust as they quickly informed me that it had been cured previously and could hang for up to a year. I tried not to think about this as I took a big chunk of the meat and stuffed it into my bread.

Gareth tells me that the big pylons at the back of the Finca run up from Riba-Roharja and that, until the Englishmen arrived, the villagers were using generators running on diesel, or candles for lighting and fires for heating and cooking. At first, the villagers appeared outraged that the pylons were up and sent Juanes to enquire if they would all die of cancer because of them, or if they would cause fires in a storm. To be honest, they do look imposing and are an eyesore amongst the surrounding beauty. It did not take long though for the neighbours to see the benefits and David said that people walk in to the Finca and take great delight in flicking all the light switches on, or turning the knobs on the cooker until the rings burned red. Three months after the pylons went up, Juanes was the first to have the electricity put into his house, and within the year all the other neighbours had followed suit.

Gareth, removing his t-shirt in the mid-day heat and wrapping it haphazardly around his head, tells me that next time I am in Valencia I must bring the family to one of their dinner parties. The couple entertains quite a lot and invites their friends from Valencia, as well as the neighbours. I smile as I picture the scenario. David and Gareth have some flamboyant friends in town and I imagine them mingling with the other residents of Los Vinos Manos, most of whom never venture further than Riba-Roharja or, at a push, Chiva. These places are visited on the back of a donkey. I also think of the mess my children could cause to their immaculate home. If I do take them up on their kind offer, I will also demand a detailed map. A repeat performance of my journey here, complete with my children in the back of the car, would not cause me to drive off the mountain, but to voluntarily jump from it.

I am pleased that the villagers were more concerned with their modern way of living rather than their personal life and I believe that both men have brought a great deal to Los Vinos Manos. They have enhanced life for the villagers and managed to become part of their small community. I thank them both for their hospitality and openness. I spend another 10 minutes walking around and taking pictures, perhaps delaying the drive until Gareth, my knight in shining armour, tells me that I can follow him back to Riba-Roharja because he wants to see a friend there. I kiss David on the cheek, thank him and promise to email a copy of my life writing project for him to read. It's time for me to leave this beautiful place and while making my way back to the tin I promise myself I will return.

Gemma Middleton

Solange

She felt dead. Lifeless. Solange's eyes flickered open reluctantly. She reached for the alarm clock – set for 6am, but redundant now – and turned it off. She didn't have to get up just yet. Another 20 minutes to luxuriate in misery before the day began in earnest and the demands of caring for Mrs Jackson crowded out her troubled thoughts.

Grey Wiltshire light seeped through the drawn curtains. She could make out the familiar furnishings by heart. In the corner, a large tallboy oozing mothball fragrance. On the far wall, a chair and lamp – solid reminders of the money the Jacksons had enjoyed. In the centre of the room, her four-poster that smelled of age but sat with ease in the centre of two rattan rugs. It was sparse, almost comfortable. No mirrors, but why should a carer need a mirror? No flowers either, but why should there be? She was here to do a job; to look after the old lady for six weeks. This was an opportunity to earn some money and send it home to the children until she had a better idea of how best to support them all.

She shouldn't feel sorry for herself. She shouldn't feel belittled. And she didn't, most of the time. But as her gaze shifted to the alcove, she couldn't hold back the tears any longer. There it stood in blue enamel disdain; the water bowl and pitcher presented to her upon arrival at the manor house as "the only place servants have permission to wash themselves." Tears sliding, she sank beneath the covers one last time. Just for a moment she would remember yesterday and the farm in Zimbabwe.

"I want to marry you," Paul had said. "I want to make you happy. I want to take away your pain and look after you and the children, Solange. I've never loved Anna, stayed with her for the sake of habit alone. She'll understand. Please. Please let me look after you?" So she did. Against her better judgement and in agonising guilt, she did. Because Paul had been her friend. And because she wanted to feel whole again.

The wedding was lovely; emerald lawns and banksia rose the perfect foil for a lakeside wedding with family and friends. Huge spits of roasting pig lit up the October night. Music wafted gaily between the bobbing fez and bow-tie clad servants as they served round upon round of cocktails and snacks and "isn't this so wonderful, sir's" into the pre-dawn cicada sky. Beneath the canvas awning, friends locked other-side-of-the-room glances, smiled with benevolence and breathed a collective sigh of relief that at long last Solange would be happy.

"Such a tragic life she's had, losing her parents like that ... their own aircraft too ... then her little girl (heart defect it was) ... and then her husband killed in a boating accident only a year later. Poor thing. It's all been too much for her. So wonderful she can make a new start now ..."

The tiniest misgivings they felt as Paul lifted his glass and turned to Solange with a barely audible "Now you belong to me" would surely dissipate in the headiness of the occasion. And so they danced and laughed and twittered with forced exuberance to make it so.

Ignoring Anna's throwaway jibe that she was welcome to Paul and his "cruelty that knows no bounds" as the histrionics of a spurned wife, Solange set about making 'Two Rivers' a haven. Flowerbeds were planted with roses, hydrangeas, wisteria, bougainvillea. Lawns were planted where before there had been only red-clay waste. Topiaries and archways made playful backdrop for water features and bird sanctuaries. Servants hummed joyfully in the white-starched aroma of fresh breads and pastries churned out by wood-fired furnaces. And the farm labourers grew to love her fiercely – called her 'Nkosi mama'. Daily they brought for her inspection and approval the crocheted twine mats they had made from her gifts of embroidery string. They waited for her every morning when she walked to the compound of huts at the southern end of the farm and chatted animatedly to her about their lives over hot, sugary tea and maize meal porridge. Paul busied himself on the lands. He planted, reaped and cured his tobacco with supervisory aplomb and taught the children to hunt and fish and ride. Solange felt safe again. Peaceful. Secure in the knowledge that she had married a good man who would protect her and the children.

But it didn't last. Paul changed. He began to criticise. First, the children – for not being able to shoot properly or bait a line quickly enough. Then the servants – for not displaying due reverence in their duties to "serve, be seen, but never heard". And lastly, Solange – for almost everything. She was too lenient with the children. She had too many friends. She wasn't grateful enough. Spent too much time chatting to the farm workers. Had too much money.

In March 1999 he introduced a household rule. Bedtime was regulated so that lights were out by 9pm. No one was exempt from his draconian law and even the farm generator quietened in obedience at precisely 8.55pm. In the shadowy half-light of their bedroom, as the house stilled in silence, Paul's Jekyll became Hyde. From his "little black book of memory" he called to account the daily wrongdoings of the family. Recalling with whispered menace, every transgression, he ended the nightly tirade with demands for change. Food must *not* be taken without permission. Laughter *must* be controlled. Solange must put him first in *all* things.

Soon, wider restrictions followed. Rules were imposed that neither Solange nor the children dared breach. They were not allowed to leave the farm without him, which meant that visits to friends or trips to the local store became impossible. On the odd occasion she had permission to drive the children to school (a task now allotted to the farm driver), Paul would call her mobile phone every quarter hour. The farm gates were kept permanently locked – his, the only key. Telephone calls were monitored. Visitors were not allowed. He would not be questioned and argued with icy calm that the family needed a return to 'obedience'. Reward and punishment became the order of the day. If she behaved and did as she was told, she was rewarded. If not, he punished her. In various ways and with varying degrees of cruelty. "Your children are too dependent on you Solange" he told her "and I've decided to take action. Monique is too old to be living at home. She must move out." Solange cried. Begged. Pleaded with him that Monique was only seventeen. And was punished. Paul announced that Monique would be sent to school in England within the month, rather than at the end of the term. When Solange refrained from weeping inconsolably at the airport, Paul rewarded her with a visit to a friend.

As quietly as the July frost that wraps its icy tendrils around the newly planted seedlings, there fell upon the farm and its inhabitants a gripping despair. Solange found solace in sleep, her afternoon siesta stretching sometimes into early evening oblivion. The children stayed in their rooms. Servants padded lightly about the house, their former gaiety replaced with sorrowful sighs and shakings of the head as they gathered in teatime discontent. This was not good.

The madam did not deserve this. The children would not grow well with such a father. Joy and laughter were gone. In their place, an all-pervading quiet – broken only by malevolent footsteps along the barbed wire fence of the security guards trained to "keep an eye on the madam."

In August Paul approached her. The farm was losing money. Tobacco prices had fallen, the economy was unstable and he needed Solange to invest her inheritance in the farm. Besides, he had done enough. He had provided a roof for her children and honour to her status. It was a shock. The money she had was for her children - hard-earned savings Solange had put aside for their education and future. Besides, the country was in turmoil and security of tenure for any farmer in grave doubt.

Robert Mugabe was in retribution mode. Robbed of the referendum vote that would have increased his powers – made him President for life, legalised abortion and outlawed foreign citizenship – his quest to destroy the white man's privilege became all-consuming. War veterans had begun to move onto former settler farms. Young, militant and the mouthpiece for his vengeance, the veterans began a tirade of attacks on white-owned farms. Night-time raids, theft and intimidation became the norm. Huge groups of government-paid thugs moved onto properties countrywide and set up a base. On Paul's farm, destruction was rife. Trees were chopped down for firewood. The dairy herd was slaughtered needlessly. Arable tobacco lands were taken over for makeshift housing. The farm labourers were forced to attend rally meetings and bribed with the promise of the white man's land. Guns were pointed in the face of those brave enough to resist and many injured or killed in the attempt. How could Solange contemplate pouring precious savings into the open cesspool of imminent land acquisition? It wasn't right. Surely Paul would not expect her to invest? Surely?

But he did. He insisted upon it and told her that unless she invested he would send all the children to England. Even when the war veterans had turned upon the family the full force of once-loyal labourers - infiltrated the mindset of her beloved Shonas with their quiet, peaceable hearts and turned them into an angry mob – he demanded it. Neither the "leave or die" chants from the compound or the clenched fist slogans tied to every tree changed his mind. Such was the power of his persuasion that Solange finally acquiesced. To do otherwise would have been impossible. For just as the war veterans had embarked upon a systematic wearing down of the fighting spirit of their enemy, so had Paul. In July 1999, her savings accounts were transferred into his name, her offshore portfolio liquidated and her assets refunded by way of a cheque made out to him. Title deeds to her former home were signed over. Two weeks later they had to leave the farm.

He didn't fight to keep it. He didn't try to find recompense within the law. Merely shrugged when the police commissioner arrived to say the farm had been sectioned and repossessed and then handed over the keys to his life without a backward glance. In December he took the family to a new home in the city; one where rules and regulations were enforced with the same intensity. Her beloved animals were sent to the pound. Her furniture was sold off as excess to the requirements of a smaller house. Her books, documents and collection of precious letters were burned in the flames of his petulance. Nothing important to her was kept. All traces of her former life were obliterated. And a year later she left him.

Dispirited and penniless, she moved out of the house and into a rented cottage. He didn't fight to keep her, either. What he fought to keep was her money. With it, he purchased a five-bedroom house. Then, a security business in the heart of the city, a new car and a holiday. Finally, he purchased a divorce.

She wanted to die. She wanted not to feel any more. She wanted the oblivion of the other side; the warm ethereal reunion with her loved ones that death would bring. Divorce from Paul had brought separation from her children. Unable to earn enough to pay bills or cope with the rising rate of inflation, she had had to leave Zimbabwe – leave her children with a friend and fly to England to do care work for the elderly. No longer mistress of all she surveyed, no longer guardian of a sun-kissed veldt, her life now was meaningless. It had become a hand-to-mouth existence where every precious penny earned was sent back to Africa. Once prosperous and carefree, once mother and wife, she was now just a servant in first-world anonymity - her children left behind in a country in economic meltdown.

Moving aside the bedclothes, Solange sat up slowly. Inside her overnight bag were pills; the ones prescribed by the doctor in Harare just before she left two weeks ago. A mixture of tranquilisers, sleeping pills and the odd painkiller she had pilfered from the tray in Mrs Jackson's armoury of preventatives, a handful or two would be enough to end it all. But first she would write to the children. First, she would tell them she loved them and ask them to forgive her this desperate step. And then she would make breakfast for Mrs Jackson.

Michelle Burton

A Good Night Out.

I have often wondered at the interpretation of a 'good night out.' On many occasions I have relayed to friends a raucous Saturday evening, but no matter how much enthusiasm I inject into my portrayal, I never quite manage to capture the feelings of hilarity that the event brought upon me. After listening intently to a conversation between two students in the union bar, I know where I am going wrong. I obviously place too much emphasis on how funny and amusing the evening was and I must have the wrong idea of what constitutes a good night.

Both students were lounging across a sofa. One looked like a young Einstein, an array of hair and tiny horn-rimmed glasses lost on a chubby face. His companion looked like he belonged in a rock band, his most evident feature was his eyes, caked in thick black eyeliner, his hair also on a par with Einstein, but strategically placed with a pot of gel.

Student 1: (vigorously texting and not looking up) "Dan was like…..I'm not getting involved, bad for like….others getting involved."

Student 2: (full of admiration, an awe-struck smile on his face) "Was he like, really hammered?"

Student 1: (still texting) "Yea, like, we took photo as a memory. He was like, really disfigured man."

Student 2: (smile still stuck) "Wow! What an AMAZING night"

Student 1: (fingers showing no sign of slowing down) "The guy just sat at home for like, two weeks, moping and feeling shit cos he like, sooo had a beating."

Student 2: (face now serious) "I would be like, so embarrassed, if I got smacked in front of my mates. What a pisser."

Student 1: (slight pause of finger movement) "Yea, we have some awesome nights out. Wanna come with us on Saturday? Ever been to Bristol?"

At this point I thought student two was ready to declare his undying love and affection for student one. I prayed for the rest of the afternoon that the wind didn't change and student two would be stuck grinning like a village idiot for the rest of his natural life.

Gemma Middleton

Why didn't I tell him?

I have dreaded this day; it has been marked on the calendar in a big black circle that matches the cloud hanging over me. I just want it to be over, to hide away, but I need to carry on for the sake of the children.

I phoned but they said that he is not back from theatre yet. It seems to be taking so long.

The days and weeks seem to have passed by so quickly and have turned into years. We have grown up and out together. My hair is going grey and his is gone altogether. So why then didn't I just tell him? He has been at the 'business end' during the birth of each of our children. He has seen parts of me I have no desire to know. Yet still I left so much unsaid.

I'm going to phone back in an hour and a half. Why is it taking so long?

People keep saying that I'm being so brave. I want to reply "What choice do I have?" But I don't. I just say that I am fine and things are fine. If I keep saying it I might believe it. People want to help, they really care, but what can they do? Their eyes are full of pity. Does that mean mine are showing how petrified I am? Part of me wants to be near others, but I think I make them nervous. Then I start to get annoyed because their day is so normal.

I'm going to phone back in an hour and a quarter. Why is it taking so long?

I should have told him, let him know just how much he means to me. Why can't I just say "I love you" without following it with "...but not as much as shoes"? Why can't I gush out sonnets of sunsets and roses? Who am I kidding? He would have curled up in fits of laughter if I did. I guess that is why I love him so much. But I should have said something more than "I'll see you tomorrow, love you". Why is it that

I can talk so eloquently about my desires and ambitions but forget to mention that I need him by me?

I'm going to phone back in an hour. It shouldn't be taking this long.

The children aren't coping. Rosie looks so scared. I hadn't noticed before that her eyes are just like her father's. They are such a beautiful green, just like emeralds. She is making herself ill with worry. Why can't I take her pain away? We have made fairy cakes that look like biscuits. Josh is out the front and seems to have an interest in botany. No, that is just wishful thinking. He is suffering. He is only 13 but is trying to be 30. He doesn't really understand what is going on, but is trying to cope with a nightmare.

I'm going to phone back in half an hour. Why is it taking so long?

Dear God, I promise if everything goes alright I will stop buying so many clothes. I will stop eating chocolate and drinking red wine. I will do anything - just make it alright. I will tell him that he is my world. I want to spend the rest of my life with him and grow old with him next to me. I love him, so why the hell didn't I tell him?

I'm going to phone back now. I need to know, is there still time to tell him?

Alison Killeen

Bath

The historical city of Bath is situated in a valley where the River Avon cuts through the limestone plateau of the Southern Cotswolds. It is surrounded by countryside and is built upon the Pennyquick Fault which is host to the only source of hot mineral water in Britain. Hence the reason for Bath's famous architectural building, The Roman Baths. Modestly named by the construction designers, The Baths use the mineral water that many believe contain age-old healing properties. The Baths are no longer in use today, but the spring water is still used as a treatment at the Mineral Hospital where arthritis sufferers bathe in the hope of some release from their illness.

This Georgian city has visitors flocking from all around the world, to gaze on and admire the fascinating architecture and relish the beautiful surrounding countryside. But how much do people really see during a visit to Bath? As you stroll down the main street in the heart of the city, pretty cobblestones remind you of a time long ago. The street is full of bustling shops, boutiques and places of interest and the sounds of street entertainers amuse as you pass. But there is something else apparent to anybody looking closely enough.

Poverty. Poverty, homelessness and a drug problem to rival major cities such as Bristol. Big Issue sellers wander up and down the streets, targeting middle-class women in the hopes of selling a magazine to raise enough cash to pay for a B&B that evening. Or, like the vast majority, to spend it on drugs and alcohol, hoping to blot out the harsh facts of their lives. Beggars lie wherever they can before an irate shop manager forces them on their way. Wrapped in anything to keep them warm, often accompanied by a mongrel dog on a piece of string, and always with a badly spelt, hand-written sign asking for money, their dirty faces tell a story. I always ask myself how many visitors to the city see this, and wonder if they are too busy admiring the commercial side of the town, paying extortionate entrance fees for the chance to see a pile of rubble and stone that was once the heart of the city during the Roman era.

Many professional move to Bath, purchasing houses built in the Georgian era. Beautiful buildings that speak of wealth and prosperity - and the closer they are to the city centre, the more costly they are. The Circus is one of the most famous groups of houses in the town. Elaborate in design, it consists of three terraces of houses curved around a central circular space. It surrounds the area now known as Queens Square and was designed by John Wood the Elder in 1754. Estate Agents claim to have perspective buyers on waiting lists, desperate to purchase a house in the Circus and willing to pay big money for these properties. The reason? Because a house is not just somewhere to live but a status symbol to tell others of success and achievement in our lives.

If we travel two miles from the city centre, along the well-known London Road, we arrive at an area called Snow Hill. Here, the houses were firstly constructed as prefabs, supposedly temporary shelters erected after the Second World War for families that had lost their homes during the bomb attacks. The area began by housing families that had nothing and Snow Hill maintains the same status to this day. It is an area that has the worst unemployment figures in B&NES and reports suggest that the drug problem in Snow Hill is more extreme than in many poverty-stricken areas in Bristol. The houses are dilapidated, run down and in some cases dangerous. Many of

Bath's less fortunate families are housed here, or are third generation from the original occupants after the war. It is an area that is ignored and overlooked, despite thousands of pounds spent on restoration projects just two miles down the road in the centre, where upper-class individuals are willing to spend half a million pounds on one property in the Circus. This amount would buy them ten two bed-roomed houses in the heart of Snow Hill.

No one can deny the charm, the beauty or the history of Bath. It is a city unlike any other, if only because of the divide in social status amongst the 175,000 residents that live here or the 500,000 visitors who come every year. To me, Bath screams of ignored poverty that is as apparent now as it was 300 years ago, only today many people have little recognition that it exists.

The next time you visit this city, try and see the real Bath, looking past the preconceived ideas you may have of what the city is like. You might end up seeing more than you expect.

Gemma Middleton

All About Me

When I was a teenager I thought by the time I was 40 I would be either dead (I was going through a morbid stage) or be some power-dressing executive. Thankfully, neither is true. In actual fact, I'm in my final year of a degree. So what happened in the intervening 20 years? After leaving school I went to Art College. By the time I had finished my course I'd had enough of education and the thought of doing a degree sent me into a cold sweat. Then I got married to my wonderful husband and had our three lovely children – today they are behaving so they are lovely, it may be a different case tomorrow so I might have to edit this.

I have had various jobs over the years. When my youngest child started school I began to feel drawn towards learning again, so took an Access Course so I could apply to universities. Surprisingly, I turned out to be quite intelligent. Mind you, when I started university I struggled. It turns out that I'm dyslexic (explains a lot, like not being able to read until I was seven) but have been given excellent support.

Would I do it all again? Most definitely, with a cherry on the top. I love my degree course. Yes, it has been hard work, but I have learnt so much and writing has opened a whole new world for me. And my sensible suit with the killer shoulder pads will remain firmly at the back of the wardrobe!

Alison Killeen

Bright Whites

Always Look on the Bright Side of Life

SCENE 1
Doctor - well spoken older gentleman.

Maria - late 30s
Younger Maria – as a 12-year-old girl.
Tommy - about 12, his voice hasn't broken yet.
Teacher - 30s and harassed.
Bill - 14, his voice has broken.
John - about 16.

MUSIC: SONG FROM MONTY PYTHON'S LIFE OF BRIAN- *'ALWAYS LOOK ON THE BRIGHT SIDE OF LIFE.'* MUSIC FADES. DOCTOR SPEAKS IN A CLEAR AND PRECISE VOICE.

SCENE 1: INTERIOR OF DOCTOR'S OFFICE.

DOCTOR: Mrs Smith, you have a stage three breast cancer. It is DCIS, ductal cancer in situ. A large area of your breast is affected and I feel that the best course of treatment would be a mastectomy. This would ensure that all affected tissue is removed. Afterwards you will need a short course of radiotherapy……..

DOCTOR'S VOICE BEGINS TO FADE. AS MARIA'S VOICE COMES IN THERE IS A SLIGHT ECHO TO IT.

MARIA SMITH: (THOUGHT) I suppose I should be feeling something but I don't. He could be telling me my car has failed its MOT for all I care. John has got hold of my hand so tightly. Why isn't he looking at me? Why isn't he saying anything? He is always so strong; he can always say something that makes me feel better, that will make me *feel*. But he is not saying anything. He is concentrating on each movement of the doctor's mouth. Not taking his eyes off him. Oh, God, I think he might even be crying. Why don't I feel something? I am about to lose a breast and all I feel is empty.

PAUSE

The first time any boy noticed me was because of my breasts. I had just got this new school blouse. It was beautiful cotton, with a small collar. It was close fitted and did emphasise my developing chest.

SOUND OF A ROWDY CLASSROOM, CHILDREN MOVING CHAIRS AND SITTING DOWN.

TOMMY: Wow look, Maria's got boobs. Where've you been hiding them?

MARIA: Get lost Tommy Phillips.

HE BEGINS TO SING TO THE TUNE FROM WEST SIDE STORY

TOMMY: 'Maria, she's got a pair called Maria…'

TEACHER WALKS IN AND CLOSES THE CLASSROOM DOOR

TEACHER: Right, quieten down you lot. Settle down.

TOMMY: Look sir, Maria's got a pair of boobs.

TEACHER: This may come as a shock to you Phillips, but that is what's known as puberty and it is a well known fact that girls mature faster than boys. You are living evidence of that fact, Phillips.

JEERING FROM THE REST OF THE CHILDREN

If you could get your hormones under control we could perhaps get on with this lesson. After all this is a maths lesson, not biology. Turn to page 24 in your text books…….

CLASSROOM SOUNDS BEGINS TO FADE. SCENE 2

MARIA: (THOUGHT) Overnight I became popular. Boys were

noticing me. It made me feel good. I knew my new-found popularity was due to the fact that they were ever hopeful of a bit of under-blouse activity. Then Bill came on the scene. He was really cool. He would go round in a gang and their main aim in the lessons was to mess about. He was exactly the sort of boy my mum would hate me to go out with. And so when he asked me to go to a party with him I jumped at the chance.

PARTY SOUNDS. THE MUSIC IS 'BLONDIE - HEART OF GLASS.'

BILL: Great, there is some cider, want some Maria?

MARIA: No, I'll stick to lemonade.

BILL: Oh, for God's sake, live a little. This isn't a church youth club. I hope you'll not be like this all night?

MARIA: Like what?

BILL: Uptight and frigid.

MARIA: All I said was I didn't want a cider.

BILL: Come on let's dance.

<u>THE SOUND OF THE MUSIC GETS STRONGER AS THEY MOVE INTO THE ROOM WHERE IT IS PLAYING AND PEOPLE ARE DANCING.</u>

MARIA: So, whose party is it?

BILL: I don't know. It's a friend of Gary's sister, I think.

MARIA: Great! That makes us gatecrashers. No wonder people keep giving us funny looks.

BILL: You're doing it again, stressing. I know people here, it's OK.

MARIA: What are you doing?

BILL: Getting a bit closer. See that feels better doesn't it? You are beginning to relax now. You smell really lovely. I really like your top, especially the front. (CLOSER) I've fancied you for ages. That is a really lovely top.

<u>SFX OF KISSING. THEN MUMBLING AS MARIA PULLS AWAY</u>

MARIA: Slow down. I can hardly breathe.

<u>SFX KISSING AGAIN.</u>

No, stop. Are you trying to climb down my throat?

BILL: Maria you're so lovely, I just can't help myself. Come on, let's go upstairs it'll be quieter and we won't be disturbed.

MARIA: No. Bill, get your hands off. They're boobs, not a piece of play dough. God, if you are like this down here you've got to be joking if you think I'll go upstairs. Will you get off me?

JOHN: She asked you to leave her alone.

BILL: Yeah, well who asked you?

JOHN: (CLOSER AND MORE MENACING) Leave her alone.

BILL: Who made you Superman, defending a girl's honour? Where's your blue pants? You are welcome to her; she's as cold as a bloody iceberg.

<u>MUSIC CHANGE S TO 'SQUEEZE – TAKE ME, I'M YOURS'.</u>

JOHN: Are you OK?

MARIA: Yeah, just a bit manhandled but fine. Thanks.

JOHN: I don't think I've seen you before .. er … John Smith, like the beer.

MARIA: It's not, is it? That sounds like it's made up.

JOHN: Yeah, I know, my mum and dad weren't very inventive.

MARIA: I'm Maria Jenkins.

GIRLS VOICE, SHE IS ABOUT SIXTEEN.

GIRL: Do either of you know Bill?

MARIA: Why?

GIRL: He's thrown up all over the bathroom; my Mum's going to kill me. There are carrots all over her poodle toilet roll cover. God knows how much he has drunk.

MARIA: No, sorry I don't know him.

GIRL: (OFF) Can someone get me a bucket and some water.

MARIA: I think I had better go before I'm put on puke duty.

JOHN: I'll walk you home.

MARIA: What about the party?

JOHN: I have had enough here, it is a bit lame.

SFX: MOVING THROUGH PARTY. THEN THE

FRONT DOOR CLOSING BEHIND THEM.

EXT- FOOTSTEPS WALKING DOWN A STREET.

JOHN: So is that the end of a great love affair between you and Bill?

MARIA: If one lung-crushing kiss and a quick grope makes a love affair, then yes it is over. He seemed so cool at school but get him on his own and he is like an immature octopus.

JOHN: You're not too upset then?

MARIA: (LAUGHER IN HER VOICE) No, I'll get over it.

JOHN: (HESITANTLY) I was wondering if you would like to come to the pictures with me. *Life of Brian* is showing and I thought ....

MARIA: That would be good. When do you want to go?

JOHN: Next Saturday. I'll pick you up from.....?

MARIA: Here, this is my house.

JOHN: OK, see you next Saturday at 7.30.

MARIA: See you.

MARIA'S VOICE FADES IN.

              SCENE 3

MARIA: (THOUGHT) I can't believe how I managed to stay so cool, inside I was drooling. He was so gorgeous. His eyes were amazing, a deep blue with a twinkle that made you think he was laughing. Over the next week I tried to find out as much as I could about him. He was two years ahead of me at school; really well liked and had a large circle of friends. Apparently lots of girls fancied him. So I couldn't believe that he wanted to go out with me. (PAUSE)

On the day of the date I went shopping and bought a new outfit. I spent hours getting ready and on the dot of seven thirty he turned up. Mum managed to get to the door before me and was quizzing him. I really wished she had taken her apron off.
The film was really good and we laughed all the way through. We held hands and occasionally had a furtive glance at each other. But the

best part was the walk home afterwards.

EXT- IN A STREET

SFX- WALKING DOWN A STREET.

JOHN: That was an ace film.

MARIA: It was really funny. Did you hear that some vicars think it is blasphemous and it has been banned in Norway? Some people need to get a life.

JOHN: It's mad, it's just a joke. You have got to be able to laugh at things. The end bit was ace, with them all singing on their crosses. That's the way I think it should be, always looking for the positives.

MARIA: It's just a film, I don't think that when people were crucified that they would have had a bit of a sing song.

JOHN: I know but it's just the whole attitude of the film, laughing about things, having fun.

MARIA: So if you lost your leg you would have a good laugh?

JOHN: Yeah, I would still be able to hop about.

MARIA: What if you lost a hand?

JOHN: I'm quite attached to my right one but I could manage.

MARIA: What if you lost a testicle?

JOHN: Ouch. I could function, as it were, with just the one.

MARIA: What if you lost both?

JOHN: Now that is just cruel. It would be a bit difficult to smile but at least I would have a nice high-pitched laugh. (BEAT) I wouldn't have laughed if you said 'no' to coming out with me.

MARIA: Yeah, I bet you say that to all the girls.

JOHN: No, I don't. Well not all the girls (LAUGH) (BEAT) I haven't been able to stop thinking about you all week. The moment I saw you I fancied you.

MARIA: Yeah, I bet you say that to all the girls.

JOHN: No, you're the first. I know it sounds like a cheesy one liner but I mean it.

MARIA: That's nearly romantic.

JOHN: No one's called me nearly romantic before.

MARIA: Well I wouldn't be too impressed; I have only got the likes of Bill to go on. Are you going to kiss me then?

JOHN: Beautiful and domineering, what more could a man want?

MARIA: (THOUGHT) We have been together ever since. Grown up, had a family and I thought we would grow old and watch our grandchildren from the comfort of a rocking chair.
(BEAT) But now what?

(PAUSE) I am going to have to lose a breast so as to stop this thing that is growing in me, dictating what happens. It has come into my world uninvited, taken over my body and is silently crawling through me. I am going to be changed for ever. How will I be able to look at myself?

(BEAT. PANIC RISING IN HER VOICE) Oh my God, maybe that is why John isn't looking at me, he can't bear the thought of the way I will be. He said he wouldn't be able to laugh if he lost me, maybe that also applies to parts of me. Am I going to lose him as well as a breast?

SCENE 4

INTERIOR –BACK IN THE DOCTOR'S OFFICE, HIS VOICE BEGINS TO CUT BACK IN

DOCTOR: Have you any questions Mrs Smith?

MARIA: (DISTRACTED) What happens if I don't have the mastectomy?

DOCTOR: I am afraid the prognosis wouldn't be as good. It really is the best course of action to prevent the cancer from recurring.

MARIA: I'm not going to have it done.

JOHN: You've got to.

SFX-MARIA GETS UP AND LEAVES THE DOCTOR'S OFFICE

MARIA: (THOUGHT) I meant to walk away but my legs went weak. So I stood with my head on the door. That's when I heard the Doctor talking to John.

DOCTOR: Mr Smith I really do believe that this is the best way to tackle the cancer. It isn't something that I recommend lightly.

JOHN: I appreciate that. I'll talk to her; maybe it's just the shock. She seems so well, I don't know where this illness has come from. You just don't think things like this will happen.

DOCTOR: I know this is a big thing for you and your wife to come to terms with. But if we are going to operate it does need to be soon.

JOHN: I'll go and speak to her.

MARIA: (THOUGHT) When I heard this I quickly went to the car park.

<u>SFX-JOHN LEAVES THE OFFICE
EX-HOSPITAL CAR PARK SOUND OF DISTANT TRAFFIC</u>

JOHN: (SOUNDS OUT OF BREATH) I've been looking for you.

MARIA: (SOUNDS DISTANT) Well you have found me. I think I might take up smoking.

JOHN: What are you going on about?

MARIA: What's the worst it can do? Give me cancer?

JOHN: You have got to have the operation, weren't you listening to what the doctor said?

MARIA: Do you remember our first date, when we went to see *The Life of Brian*?

JOHN: Of course, but what the hell has that got to do with anything?

MARIA: Do you remember what you said then?

JOHN: No. It was 20-odd years ago and what has this got to do with your surgery?

MARIA: (HER VOICE BECOMING A BIT PANICKY AND LOUDER). You said you wouldn't be able to laugh if you lost me. Well I'm going to lose a part of me. And you were so dumbstruck in the doctor's office; you didn't look at me once or smile. I realized that you might not find me attractive any more and that you might stop loving me and I might lose you. (HER VOICE BEGINS TO TRAIL OFF)

JOHN: I wasn't smiling, because of what the doctor was telling us. And I'm scared; scared for what you will have to go through. D'you really think I am that shallow that I only care about the way you look? The worst part is I feel so bloody useless. I want to make it go away but I can't. As for your breast I don't care, all I want is you safe. I would trade any part of me to take your place but I can't. I love you Maria, I can't function with out you. Please have the operation.

SFX_MARIA CRYING AND THEM KISSING.

MARIA: (STILL CRYING BUT QUIETLY) You realize we will have to change the words from *Always Look On The Bright Side of Life*, to 'always look on the right side of your wife'.

JOHN: That's not funny.

MARIA: Yeah, it is.

JOHN: No, it's not.

MARIA: It is a bit; you know you want to laugh.

JOHN: (LAUGHING) It is still not funny.

MARIA: It must be, you're laughing.

THEIR VOICES FADE AND 'ALWAYS LOOK ON THE BRIGHT SIDE OF LIFE BEGINS TO PLAY.'

Alison Killeen

All About Me

So let me tell you a little bit about myself. I am (blank) years old and live in Somerset. My family consists of a partner and four children, who 'challenge' and inspire me everyday. So you may be asking yourselves: How did a blank-year-old make it to university and decide to co-write a book? The terror of Tesco's checkouts are to be praised. Inspired by the fear of being sat listening to rude customers and a monotonous bleep, I wanted to find something that would make better use of my brain. This book comes out of a second-year module in which we wanted to put together an anthology of our work from our time at university. From a small acorn has grown this volume of hard labour, which has been both a pleasure and at times an albatross dragging me down and distracting me from my familial duties.

Throughout my creative 'career' I have done my best to avoid sharing my writing in even the smallest of seminar groups. So consider how exposed (thankfully not in the literal sense) I feel by including my work in this book. It was however, quite simply too good an opportunity to let slip by. The sharing of my work for this book with my co-writers on an

almost daily basis has luckily given me a certain air of "oh what the hell."
So here it is, and…"What the hell."

Amanda Stone

The Comfort of Ariel

Nature

Nature in Periphery

Fields at dusk; intrusive commune.
Expectation hangs in moisture laden air.
Washed by the breeze, amid unseen strangers
of alien tongue.

Damp denim hems, creating a disturbance-
a scattering flight. Miracles found,
in impossible clouds, and the helical descent
of a sycamore wing.

Amanda Stone

Her

Often described as a woman,
from a man's point of view,
can be unpredictable and moody
or calm and gentle to you.

Ride her at your peril
take caution in her vastness,
soft and reassuring; 'til
she shows you her harshness.

A form of outstanding beauty
pulling you into her breast,
feed on the life inside her
surviving only at her request.

No person shall control her,
her freedom holds no bounds,
right from the beginning
we hear only her sound.

She will fight the mountains,
destroy land within her path,
take any in her way
leave echoes of her laugh.

She will allow you in her body
but be prepared to stay on top,
your vessel will not scare her
it serves to feed her crop.

If you admire her strength
and allow her to stay free,
err on the side of caution,
by the lure of the open sea.
Gemma Middleton

Hamster

Run far on constant
yellow road.
Now light calls black,
says stop.
Find right scent,
curl,
be small in soft,
and gone.

Pitches, high and low
disturb, unfurl.
Highs grasp
and pass
from scent to scent.
Soft, calls and pulls,
says go.
But pitch and scent
make untime, now.

Amanda Stone

Sunset

Night falls with an orange bang
as sienna clashes umber,
throwing into stark relief
the patient string of stars.

Earth and sky lock and hold
in dense horizon battle,
tangible meets intangible
and both succumb to darkness.

Shadow flees from shadow
in moon's revealing light,
as trees and bush surrender
to mystery in its moment.

Owls, frogs and cicadas
begin their evensong;
native drums announce the hour
and Africa slips to dreaming.

Michelle Burton

Remembrance

Early falling sun
gilding the horizon,
with heavenly glow
of blazing autumn tones.

Trees silhouetted,
stage lit from behind,
dark and surreal,
of miniature size.

Recalling green sponge,
train track on chipboard.
Baltimore – Ohio,
on the living room floor.

Recollections of childhood,
now barely remembered.
Emotions awakened,
overwhelming once more.

Far celestial sky,
of amber lit clouds.
Where seraphim wings
can surely be heard.

For, to me,
you are always,
there in the light.
Most precious sunbeam,
who left in the night.

Amanda Stone

Invisible Strings

Telling them

I'm not sure how to tell them,
I don't know what to say,
I know the words inside,
It's just finding the right way.

What if they make assumptions?
Create a different me,
No matter whom I fall in love with,
I'm still part of the family tree.

I don't want them to be shocked,
To judge the way I am,
To tell me how to live my life,
As if they give a damn.

I have a right to happiness,
To live with what feels right,
I know that I will tell them,
I just don't feel strong to fight.

So listen to my message mum,
And know how hard it is for me,
Telling you what's going on inside,
Will help me to feel free.

All I'm really asking of you,
Is just to let things be,
I guess I really want you
Just to let me live as me.

Gemma Middleton

Tread Softly

Bring laughter, on my black dog days.
Hold me close, when darkness takes me.
Try not to fix the broken parts,
but let me, still be me.

And I will walk within your walls,
tread softly in your heart,
and let you see the side of me,
that fear keeps in the dark.

Amanda Stone

You, Me and your Epilepsy

I wake to the clack, clack sound of your mouth.
The all too familiar sound cuts into my sleep.
The slowing of your breath
as the gush of fear takes hold.
You move to the place I can not go.

I touch your arm, a gesture of comfort
or is it to become a part of your foreign world.
Beads of sweat texture your brow,
your eyes showing fear that I can never know.
Then you are back, as quickly as you left.

The house is littered with paper records:
8.30, 13.45 bad, 18.20 very bad,
to be entered into the black diary.
Trying to see a pattern, find a clue.
You mark out days in little circles.

As the years move by, will the other place
get a stronger hold on you?
How many times have we been tantalized?
a promised cure, magic pill, skilful cut.
But still the darkness fills your head.

Alison Killeen

You

In your comfort-zone of silence,
with busy hands at work
on mundane chores and humdrum things
that take so little thought,
do you see the wall that changes
and grows before your eyes?
Distance, pique and apathy
new bricks that block
your view of us.

Michelle Burton

Evening meal

We sit around the dinner table
large helpings of sausage and sarcasm.
Pink Floyd accompanying our food.
Some joke unfurls, we begin to laugh,
we laugh so hard that food falls out-
juice trickles down noses.

I want to keep this moment
put it somewhere safe, in a glass jar.
On sad days I can lift the lid,
let the feeling wash over me.

The meal is finished.
We move to our separate spaces;
like ripples we spread out.
To kitchen, sitting room, bedrooms.
The instant has gone with the sausages
but happiness remains.

Alison Killeen

The Darker Side

The Waiting Room

I just sat in the chair
and waited.
I never went to his side.
No point.
He was going, anyway,
without me.
Yellow face, sallow,
looked scared.
Tiny man by then
but big, once.
Hated the game,
death.

Gemma Middleton

My Best Friend

Enjoying the warmth
of the comfort he brings,
his friendship always there
fine tunes we sing.
Together we stand
complete as one,
always there with me
we cannot be undone.
Many have tried to
break us apart,
separate our relationship,
it pulls at my heart.
I don't want to leave him,
nor spend time away,
from the one who
is with me, night and day.
He props up my life
the way only he can,
I don't really care
if you don't understand.
Leave me alone to
stay with my friend,
 on my bottle of vodka
can I truly depend.

Gemma Middleton

Patience

Thrice-weekly visits, flirting with nurses.
Giving them sweets, joke about his boxers.
Trousers folded, on padded plastic chair.

Tubes attached, where veins allow,
in arm or leg, later shunts in neck.
Dirty life out, before clean pumped in.

Wipe up the mess, and put on a smile.
Feeling light-headed; but tipping the wink.
Stubborn independence-his long drive home.

Amanda Stone

Aged

Gnarled hands in twisted tendrils,
decrepit backbone, no support.
Pissed in pants, pads all wet,
unheard comments, no retort.

Fuzzy brain, lost in time,
rheumy eyes, long ago dead.
Sleep in foetal, veins protruding,
dreams coherent inside head.

Turned over twice, sleep disrupted,
bedsores tended on stroke of twelve.
shit wiped up, masses of sinew
empty the body, no need to delve.

Roughly pulled from bed at seven,
slippers thrust on twisted feet.
Left in confusion, stuck in chair,
wait for what? There's no retreat.

Gemma Middleton

Wordless

Numbness, blanket of dark
Deep desperate void.
No plea from lips
My mask, a smile.
Cut.
Cut.
Cut.
Relief, alive again
Red patches of purpose
Drag me to reality.
Shrouded in shame.
Slash.
Slash.
Slash.
Arms a reflection
Expression of hate,
Mirroring my sadness
Luring veins, my fate.
Gouge.
Gouge.
Gouge.
Scars reminding,
Epitome of real,
Anything, anything
That help's me feel.

Gemma Middleton

My Needs

Gotta have a hit today,
can't wait no more,
one tiny prick,
then pleasure, galore.

Cursing through veins,
taking me there,
waiting in anticipation,
till I don't have a care.

Magical colours,
relief and no pain,
unaware and so still,
so much to gain.

Won't remember much soon,
my past, or my name,
numbness and tingling,
amass in one frame.

Tightening the belt,
clenching my fist,
shaking hand nervous,
awaiting this gift.

Shit, they've collapsed,
can't get in here,
too many hits,
too little fear.

Take off my shoes,
remove a sock,
entry here to heaven,
no time to feel shock.

Bright and inviting,
begging for the pin,
slowly, now carefully,
enter needle in.

Dirty bastard, I am,
scum, with no worth,
these thoughts soon leave me,
as I depart Earth.

Gemma Middleton

Time

The cold chaps his hands in January.
Frost hurts his chest in February.
The wind bites through his trousers in March.
Throughout April- his feet are constantly wet.
May, sometimes has the flu.
Visitors come in June, sighing with sorrow.
Hot nights and days in July.
Dehydration during August.
September. The best. Nothing to endure.
October brings the headaches.
Sheltering in the doorways through November.
December. Snow next. Pretty on a Christmas card.
Might kill him, maybe.
New calendar, New Year.
Without him, if he's lucky.

Gemma Middleton

Funeral Home

Whispering, flickering, swirling in dance,
candlelight shapes your earthen shell.
Once bright, then dull, now bathed in hue
of fireglow orange-red.
Your blue-glass eyes watch wistfully,
from silent, lonely sleep;
hard box, soft lace,
surrendered hands,
Companions in this place.

Michelle Burton

Necessity

I see her in the darkened alley,
Clothes showing, baring all,
except her soul.
Legs, thigh, boots up high,
big heels. Cause pain if you desire.

Hair pulled tight, enhancing lines of life,
pouting red lips, painted to perfection.
Eyes dead, but bright outside,
Hues of purples and blues,
the clown who has to entertain.

Sauntering up and down,
needs to get paid tonight,
money for the kids, food,
the partner with powerful hands.
No tears. Too late for that.

She sees him. He beckons. She goes.
Better to pay than just take.
He has needs too.
Lady of the night.
Borne of necessity.

Gemma Middleton

Woman

Witch
bitch
whore
harlot

playing the naming game.

Mother
sister
daughter
wife

labels all the same.

Eve
Lilith
Hera
Clytemnestra

always got the blame.

Persecute
demonise
prostitute
sacrifice

say the scapegoat's name.

Amanda Stone

24 Hours

24 hours in a mundane life,
capping of roles from student to wife.
Real and whimsical vying for lead,
'should I settle to chores or sit down to read?
Lose myself in the world of literal,
practice routine at the cost of mythical?'

Choices wage war, then finally concede,
the twin petitions of want and need
can exist and conclude without much ado,
perchance they join forces the whole day through.
And so I resolve, with cheerful conviction,
indeed the banal can inhabit the fiction.

The remainder of hours slide easily by,
my organised efforts giving the lie
to thoughts and emotions that take me away
from the simple humdrum of my everyday day.
And alongside the basic, necessary tasks
Are complex hypotheses the inner me asks,

Of life, its workings, the journey we take,
in the miniscule moment we are given to make
a difference, a change, in this sad world of powers,
in myriad clusters of 24 hours.

Michelle Burton

My place

She is the month of April
Bringing spring with rain,
she is my open garden
in her rough terrain.

Surrounding her, a border
of flowers, warm and bright,
continually they bloom
throughout day and night.

Withering and writhing
stems, reaching out to reassure,
she is my secret place
but I never realized, before.

Goats feeding on her grass,
plants growing in her earth,
birds circle in her open sky,
all appreciate her worth.

Her presence is an elm,
tall, strong and robust,
many branches reaching
up to untouched lust.

There is a special flower
a daisy by her side,
as a constant presence,
I'm standing, full of pride.

Many things are hidden here,
of secrets buried deep
under mud lay rotted plants
destroyed from tears she'd weep.

But growing are the new buds,
through death, become re-born,
she has other breathing life
to nurture through their scorn.

Gemma Middleton

A Thank You to Austen

My childhood escape,
where I danced with Astaire.
In my fantasy-land,
I was friends with Jane Eyre.

                                                                                                                                         The cruelty of youth-
                                                 my mercenary art:
tripping up Cyd Charisse,
stealing Rochester's heart.

A taste for the bad boys,
would piss off my mother.
So discovered the biker,
that worked like no other.

                                      Stereotypical female,
soon thinking of settling down.
I looked about for a good guy,
and the chance to move uptown.

A shoulder to cry on,
a nice cup of tea,
but between the sheets,
a bad boy's for me.

                        Mr Darcy's the best combination,
But where would I find such a man?
Though on earth you just can't locate him,
    with Austen you know that you can.

Amanda Stone

Large Alien

There is a large alien in the house
it has taken over a room.
It moves around all arms and legs;
drags limbs, bangs and barges.
Underneath feral hair, a face.
Awkward skin, an occasional grin.

Rarely does it speak, just grunts.
From beneath its door
strange beats, sickly smells.
It encounters its fellow beings
through internet connections;
e-mails continue through the night.

It feeds on an even diet
of burnt toast and chocolate cereal.
I do not recall when it arrived-
can't remember the day.
It has a certain enduring charm.
Strange; it reminds me of a boy, in a way!

Alison Killeen

Childhood

Miniature woman walking by.
Her mask of maturity - the painted eye.
Midriff revealed and legs on show;
With over-styled hair, where plaits used to go.
Run home little girl, go back to your toys.
Play with your friends and forget about boys.

Amanda Stone

Boy with the Blue Eyes

I remember the day you cried
because you never wanted to leave my side.
Now you are as big as me
you know exactly what you want to be.

I remember days of wheezing breath.
Your side at night I never left.
Blue eyes are still the same,
they show some of your inner pain.

Now I'm not the one you chose to tell,
your daily news, when things go well.
A father's son you will always be
but save a place just for me.

Alison Killeen

Shoes

I remember the red patent leather,
the smell and the touch and the feel,
my pride in their shine and their redness,
as I turned and I tapped and I twirled.
Time brought inevitable scratches,
and tears at the loss of their shine.
But I remember the red patent leather,
and the feeling when they were mine.

Amanda Stone

Boyhood

They live on a housing estate outside the town;
he assembles his heap of twigs.
Sometimes the ball shoots into the sky,
and he's tired of horseback chases.
Thoughts burst out like a swarm of bees,
with purpose that makes him victor.
They will never be famous hunters;
he suspects it is just pretence.
Beside him, his wife looks tired and cross;
next door, a new couple arrive.
I'm teaching him Greek, says Theo,
and right then he thinks of Aunt Annie.

Michelle Burton

Cease-fire

Quarrelsome sisters
briefly united,
splash, shriek,
grin at the camera,
sea brightened eyes,
strike a pose.
Underwear soaked,
a commando ride home.
Towels rubbing;
now suddenly cold.
Tears and tantrums
and sand between toes.

Amanda Stone

"The best time for planning a book is while you're doing the dishes."

(Agatha Christie)

"When I was little, the most thrilling words in the language were: 'Once upon a time…'"

(Mary Higgins Clark)